Thanks once again to Madison Kopp for keeping my covers from being disasters. If you're as obsessed with her as I am, you can check out the other things she's doing at @riddlemethisreads on Tiktok!

Content Warnings on Page 243

Nonymous

Nonymous

To Rue,
Who makes me feel more myself than I ever thought possible <3

Nonymous

Nonymous

Nonymous

Nonymous

A Brief History of Sky Eaton & The Blue Roof Girl

Nonymous

There was once a girl who was switched at birth.

Her name was Skye Eaton and she had absolutely no proof to confirm this, but Skye was not the type of girl stopped by something as inconsequential as logic. Skye Eaton was switched at birth simply because she had decided that she had been.

She came out bald and loud, eyes a blue that would eventually shift to a colour she'd come to call brown. This was inaccurate. Skye's eyes were a dark gold ringed with lines of green, but one wouldn't know that unless they got close enough to notice. One day, someone would.

Skye—baby Skye, swapped Skye—screamed and cried and kicked in those first early moments of her life but no one noticed that she couldn't possibly belong to mild mannered Mr. and Mrs. Eaton, bus driver and bakery owner extraordinares, because all human children screamed and cried and kicked. Skye just never stopped.

She was the kind of toddler who threw toys at walls and windows and foreheads. The kind of kindergartener who laughed out loud at jokes that she told herself in her head despite the teachers' shushing because she already knew that she was infinitely more interesting than anything they'd ever be able to tell her. If a girl tripped her at soccer, she'd tackle her to the grass. If a boy took her toy at recess, she'd scream at the top of her lungs until she got it back. She trained her dolls in battle mechanics and told stories of fire and adventure and destruction because princesses had never quite suited her.

Skye Eaton wasn't the daughter of a bus driver and baker. From the moment she'd be been born—to someone else. An astronaut or wrestler or mad scientist—Skye had been destined for things bigger than her own skin.

One day, she'd come to tell someone all of this. One day, her theory would be met with stories of fairies and changelings, beings taken and switched. She'd learn about parents leaving their imposter children in the woods and joke about the irresponsibility in that because one day, she'd be too old to believe in fairies. She wouldn't say it out loud then, maybe she wouldn't ever, but she'd go home that night and research them. Because one day, she'd be too old to believe in fairies, but maybe that day wasn't actually there quite yet. She'd think of the shadows that she occasionally caught in her parents' eyes and think about how her skin sometimes felt so tight that her very bones itched and think: *maybe I was meant for the forest after all.*

But Skye didn't know any of that yet. She hadn't begun to consider magic or forests or the girl who would teach her to love both.

She was a baby and she was switched at birth and she could make something true just by willing it to be. That was all that mattered.

Nonymous

On A Rock Thrown Over the Hedge and Against the O'Brian's Wall:

Who are you?

There was once a girl who was in trouble.

This was not new. The way Skye saw it—or maybe the way that the adults around her did—she was in a constant state of trouble. This time was just noticeable enough that she was in the office for it.

"What happened?" The secretary, a woman with thin, wired glasses and thinner, wirier fingers, asked.

There was no "why are you here?" or "who are you?" or "who sent you?" because at ten, Skye Eaton had already earned celebrity status in that office.

She shrugged at the secretary, shoved her fists into the pocket of her hoodie, and sat down to wait to see the principal.

Skye was not unaccustomed to being in the office and no one was unaccustomed to seeing her there, but she still found herself sinking a little in her seat when the announcements finished and a steady stream of students started arriving to hand in attendance folders. It would have made more sense to send Skye's class's along with her, but Skye was not the kind of student who got volunteered for such things. Maybe Mrs. J had assumed she'd eat it on the way to the office.

Stephanie Kelter had been there to see her get called down the moment the bell had finished ringing, so Skye made a point of meeting her eye when she rushed past her to hand in the folder. They'd done soccer together when they were children. Or art camp or ballet, but maybe that was Skye's memory editing itself because she couldn't remember them ever sharing a hobby. They'd been friends by proximity for a while. Two years ago,

Stephanie would have noticed her sitting there and, in all of her eight-year-old optimism, would have seen her as something that could be fixed with a smile and a "please don't get in trouble before recess, okay?"

Stephanie refused to look at her. Skye rolled her eyes and went back to sulking.

"Skye?" Principal Mitchell eventually came out of his office after what was, in Skye's opinion, far too short a wait. She had a spelling test to try and miss. "Come in."

Principal Mitchell had a diploma on the wall beside a picture of his family: him, his wife, two blond grinning kids, and golden retriever. Principal Mitchell knew nothing of birth switching or changelings or how dangerous the thick skinned, thick waisted, brown-haired being across form him was, so he held out his little glass bowl of mints and waited for Skye to take one.

Skye didn't like mints. She did like showing back up to class sucking on candy that no one else had been privy to. She pocketed it.

"How are you doing?"

Skye nodded instead of responding, waiting to be filled in. For once, she could not pinpoint what kind of trouble she'd supposedly gotten herself into.

Principal Mitchell sighed. "We have a no bullying policy here, Skye."

The girl frowned. Her eyes bunched all the way together as she did because she hadn't yet learned how to turn down her emotions. "I don't bully people."

She didn't. She hit Connor Burke for trying to cheat off her math test and getting her blamed for it then screamed at May Sandoval when she reported him for it. She threw a soccer ball at Marco Gomez when he wouldn't let any girls on his team in gym class and scratched Lainey Griffith's arm when she told Tessa Grant that Tommy Banks would never marry her after she got glasses. Skye Eaton's anger was always big and explosive, but never repetitive enough to be bullying.

"That extends past actual students," Principal Mitchell elaborated.

"I don't bully people." She had screamed at a substitute teacher the week before when she'd made the mistake of asking if there were 'any strong boys who could help stack the chairs', but that still didn't count as bullying.

The principal sighed again. He was an ever-sighing man, but maybe Skye only remembered him that way because she was the cause of most of it.

"The O'Brians have been complaining about someone trespassing on their property. Your teachers say they've heard you spreading rumours about their girl."

Even at ten, Skye already knew virtually everyone in town. Everyone did. So even though he didn't name the girl and she'd never heard of the O'Brians before, she knew. There was only one person in town truly worth getting in trouble over.

"I don't trespass," she said. "I throw."

Tied Around a Stick Found in a Cracked Bird Bath:

Who are you?!?!?!!?!?!?!

There was once a weary principal who said, "Skye. It has to stop."

There was once a maybe-girl who said "it will."

It wouldn't.

Nonymous

On a Ball Bounced Off of the Kitchen Window at 7am:

WHO ARE YOU

There was once a ten-year-old liar sitting across from a weary principal who knew better than to trust anything she said.

Principal Mitchell sighed again.

"If you keep spreading rumours—"

"Do you know her name?" The liar interrupted.

"I'm not sharing personal information with students."

It meant no.

Nonymous

On a Letter in the Mailbox:

Who are you who are you who are you who are you who are you who are you who are you who are you WHO ARE YOU

There was once a girl who was not a bully and never would be. It was extremely important that no matter what the adults in her life misunderstood about her, they at least got that right.

"It's not bullying, you know. It's just talking."

"You've been telling people she's a cyborg!" Her principal exclaimed, finally giving up on sighing.

Skye smiled. She'd always preferred this flavour of disappointment. The kind that didn't hide.

"You told people you had proof that she was from space!"

The girl shrugged. "In what world are those not compliments?"

Nonymous

Hidden Under the Doormat, Found Years Later:

Who is she?

There was once again a sighing principal. "I've talked to her parents. I think it'd be best if you wrote an apology letter."

"Okay."

"And the rumours stop."

"Okay."

"And the trespassing."

"Throwing."

"The throwing then."

"Sure."

He slid the liar a paper, pencil, and envelope.

"What's her name?" Skye stopped him when he tried to make his escape.

"Excuse me?"

"For the letter?"

The man sighed. "Just tell her you're sorry."

He left. He should have known better than to leave her alone.

Nonymous

On 12 Paper Planes, Scattered Across the Backyard:

Tell me what you are.

There was once a mysterious girl in a blue roofed house. Skye first saw her when she was eight. She was still trouble back then—too loud and too funny and too confident—but the other girls in her class hadn't yet learned to see that as anything but entertaining so their parents let a group of them meet up in the field behind their school every Friday to keep in touch over the summer. She'd been tracking the beach ball that they were trying to keep in the air when she saw her. Somehow, she already knew that it was the kind of thing she'd have to remember. She didn't know that it would be years before she or anyone outside of that blue roofed house ever saw that Blue Roof Girl again, but she was already committing her to memory.

Long blonde hair in a long, perfect braid. A Cinderella t-shirt that Skye had already decided that kids their age were becoming too old to wear, but Blue Roof Girl apparently hadn't yet. A smile with a tooth missing beaming down at her from the window.

Blue Roof Girl caught her looking and waved so Skye waved back, letting the ball fall to the ground.

"Hey!" Stephanie protested. "You didn't even try!"

"There's a kid up there." She pointed to the window, but Blue Roof Girl was already gone. The pink curtain filled the space that she'd just occupied.

Skye didn't jump to conspiracy. Not yet. She wasn't interested because she thought that there was some big secret surrounding Blue Roof Girl, she was just curious because she was new. She wanted to secure her as a friend before she got to school

in September and realized that Skye wasn't prime friendship
material. She looked back to where her parents were busy talking
with the other girls' guardians and handed the ball back to
Stephanie.

"We're going to ask her to play," she announced.

"We should—"

Skye was already gone.

Blue Roof Girl's house was easy to find once she entered
the street. It looked like it'd been built in a different era than
everything around it—though earlier or later, Skye would never
figure out. It was blue and white where everything else was red and
rust so when she knocked on the door, she was absolutely certain
that she was standing in front of the right house.

"Hello?" The man who opened the door seemed
confused to find an elementary schooler on his doorstep.

"I'm Skye." She held out a hand. "We're playing in the
field. Does your daughter want to come?"

He looked inside the house. "Sorry, you must have the
wrong address."

He started to close the door, but Skye pushed herself
through. "I don't. I saw her in the window. She—"

"Skye!" Her father, running down the street. Her friends
and their parents in tow. Skye's father caught up to her and pulled
her out of the doorway. Her feet had already been on their rug.

"You don't just—" he started to scold her, then his
attention shifted to Blue Roof Man. Or, apparently, Mr. O'Brian.
"I'm so sorry. I don't know what—"

"I was inviting the girl to play," Skye informed him. He'd tried his best to raise her to be kind and inclusive. She thought he would be happy that she'd at least gotten one of those things right.

Mr. O'Brian chuckled. "I think she's got the wrong house."

"I'm sorry," her father said again.

"No big deal," he handed her back her ball. "Have fun girls."

Maybe Skye would have believed him. Maybe. But when school started two weeks later and she was finally back in that yard again, the thin pink curtains had been replaced with blackouts. And so, she knew.

Delivered to Sadie O'Brian in a Sealed Envelope

Dear ~~robot? Alien? Spy?~~ *Blue Roof Girl,*

Now I know youve been getting my letters.

Who are you? What's wrong with you?

-    *Skye*

There was once a girl who'd believed with ever single one of her atoms that the mysterious girl in the blue roofed house was real. It just took getting in trouble for her to finally get the confirmation that she'd been longing for.

No parents apologized to her once the school told them, though. There was no "we're sorry we didn't believe you, Skye."

Just a quiet "that poor thing" and quieter disapproval.

Delivered to Sadie O'Brian in an Unsealed Envelope:

Dear Blue Roof Girl,

    I'm very very sorry I didn't respect your privasy and that I spread rumors about you even though you didn't actualy hear any of those rumors becuase you refuse to leave your house. I'm sorry my first letter wasn't actualy an apology. I promise to leave you alone and hope you can forgive me.

Your friend,
Skye

There was once a girl in a blue-roofed house who never wrote back to Skye. That just made her more interesting. Skye learned how to talk about her in secret.

She'd only share her conspiracy theories with her most trusted confidants. She'd switch rumors out for "quick write assignments" and never mention her by name, but everyone knew that none of her stories were fictional.

She stopped with the hurled notes. There was no point demanding answers from someone who refused to give them.

Found Tucked into the Inner Fold of an Unsealed Envelope:

Why did you snitch on me????? I didnt even write anything rude. Stop trying to get me in trouble just becuase your too wierd to go to school or ill break your stupid window next time. Its not my fault you don't have any friends

i was really hoping you wouldnt be this boring,
Skye

There was once a middle schooler who was finally beginning to realize why it had been so important to the faculty that she stopped theorizing about a mysterious housebound stranger.

Adults looked at people like Blue Roof Girl and thought of terminal illness before ghost stories. She'd never owned up to anything but the two official notes that she'd sent, and Blue Roof Girl's parents kept refusing to acknowledge their daughter's existence to anyone else, so it wasn't like she could apologize. She tried to move on.

And by the time the O'Brians had a change of heart, she almost had.

"We have a very special project today," her seventh grade language arts teacher announced. "There's a girl your age in our community who's too sick to leave her house, but that doesn't mean we can't all reach out to help her feel a little less alone. Her parents contacted me and asked if a few of you would wants to be penpals with her, so we're all going to brush up on our letter writing skills and reach out."

She went on to list some of Blue Roof Girl's attributes to 'inspire them'. She had a pet cat and loved animals. She liked to read. She loved fairy tales. Skye paid attention to none of it.

That was it. The chance to talk to the mysterious girl from the blue roofed house that she'd been waiting for for years. And the confirmation that there had never been any mystery at all. She'd just been antagonizing a severely ill stranger.

They were getting marked on their email writing skills because neither the O'Brians nor the faculty had stopped to consider that that wasn't how pre-teens actually communicated. Skye normally tried her best to adhere to project guidelines to make sure that she didn't give her teachers anything else to hold against her, but what could she possibly write?

An apology, maybe. But middle school Skye was allergic to apologizing. So, she spent the period pretending to write, whispering the name on the board to figure out how it tasted on her tongue.

Sadie O'Brian, Blue Roof Girl.

Sadie O'Brian.

From: Skye
To: Sadie

Hi.

- *Skye*

There were once twenty-three twelve-year-olds waiting for emails.

"I'm sure it'll mean a lot to Sadie to hear from you all!" Their teacher had said. "Make sure to let us know if anyone gets a response."

Their teacher would ask about it again and again every day that week, but apparently, Blue Roof Girl hadn't wanted pen pals after all.

From: Sadie
To: Skye

Hi.

Nonymous

Nonymous

Skye

Nonymous

From: Sadie
To: Skye

You're rude.

From: Sadie
To: Skye

And annoying.

From: Skye
To: Sadie

R u dying?

From: Sadie
To: Skye

Not any faster than you are.

From: Skye
To: Sadie

R u sick?

From: Sadie
To: Skye

No.

From: Sadie
To: Skye

Then I'm not sorry.

Skye fucking hated offices. She was used to them (probably more familiar with them then even the most overachieving of assholes) but she still hated them. They were sterile and cramped and the chairs were always uncomfortable. She was pretty sure that that last part was intentional. A way to try and get people like Skye to never want to come back. Despite her familiarity with offices, as she sat in the guidance room, waiting for her appointment to start, her leg bounced relentlessly against the tile floor.

If you asked anyone else in the building, they would tell you that Skye Eaton wasn't afraid of anything. Maybe they'd even tell you that that was where all her problems started.

No one had ever bothered actually fact checking that with Skye.

"Ah," the guidance counsellor (Skye hadn't caught her name when she'd booked the appointment and it felt rude to ask now. Despite claims to the contrary, Skye was rarely intentionally rude to teachers. Not until they deserved it.) finally arrived three minutes late. "Good to see you, Skye."

"I need references," she said. They were already three minutes behind schedule. She figured that that necessitated skipping small talk. "For some of my university applications."

"It's September," Unnamed Guidance Counsellor pointed out. "You won't even be able to apply for—"

"But I'll need them, right?"

The counsellor considered, then nodded. "For a few programs, yes. A lot of the scholarships want signatures. If you want to stay ahead of the curve, I'm sure a few of your teachers from last year would—"

"They won't," Skye said. "I already asked."

She had, multiple times. Every teacher she'd ever had since ninth grade.

"Oh." Unnamed Guidance Counsellor tapped away at her computer for a few moments. Skye wondered what she was seeing. If *'Skye Eaton, Do Not Write a Reference Letter'* was written across the top of some file somewhere. "I don't really see what you want—"

"You can make them write them, right? The whole point of high school is supposed to be getting us ready for university, so they have to—"

The woman's smile turned into a thin line. "You don't want universities getting letters from teachers who were forced to write them, Skye, trust me. Applications still don't go out for a couple of months. I'm sure some of your teachers this year will be happy to sign for you."

Skye squeezed the end of her hoodie sleeve in her fist. Moments like these required calm. She'd never been good at that.

None of her teachers would voluntarily write her anything. She already knew that. If whatever the counsellor was looking at told her anything at all about Skye, she must have known it too.

It wasn't that she wanted teachers to not like her. Things would go a lot smoother for everyone involved if they found her tolerable. They just never did.

"What about clubs? Maybe a club supervisor could—"

"I'm not in any."

The counsellor grinned. Skye instantly knew that she'd wander into some kind of trap. "There you go then! Universities are always looking for well-rounded—"

"I'm going into STEM." She didn't specify which letter of the acronym she was aiming for because she hadn't decided that part yet. "That's normally less important there if your grades are good enough."

Unnamed Guidance Counsellor's smile didn't waver. "Stuff like that changes every year. Join a club. Or even start one, I'm sure that'd look wonderful. I could give you a list of—"

"No thank you." Skye's backpack banged against the desk as she stood up. She'd already wasted eight minutes here, not including the three where she'd sat alone in silence or the fifteen she'd spent in the waiting room. She wasn't wasting any more of her morning on useless conversations. She considered popping back in to say what ever she was supposed to (probably "thanks for the help" even though the meeting had been absolutely fucking useless) but she wasn't sure if guidance counsellors counted as references. If she was going to waste her energy on looking more palatable to the adults in her life, she'd save it for the ones who could actually affect her future.

She threw her bag over her shoulder a bit more aggressively than normal as she stormed out of the office, winning her a "what the fuck!" from somewhere just beyond the door.

She winced, both relieved and not that it was just Isaac. She probably deserved Skye's shit the least, but at least she wouldn't hold any grudges over it.

"Sorry," Skye said. "You okay?"

"Took a pin corner to the shoulder, but I'll survive. You got your references?"

Skye shook her head.

"There's still time."

"Sure."

Isaac didn't get it. Isaac would never get it. She was popular and funny and despite her lower-Bs average, she'd probably end up getting into a better program than Skye on charisma alone. Skye knew that she wanted to get away too (that she probably even had more of a reason to want to) but at least she actually had the chance of doing it.

"You might get in without any," Isaac said, because she didn't get it.

Skye wasn't about to base her entire future on "might"s.

"You having the guys over tonight?" She checked.

Isaac nodded. It was tradition. On the second day of every new school year, they'd all reconvene in Isaac's backyard to roast marshmallows over their burning course outlines.

"Good," she said. "I'll meet you there."

Isaac frowned.

"What?"

"You have a plan, don't you?"

Skye grinned. "Don't I always?"

From: Skye
To: Sadie

*So high school starts tomorrow which is.... Khdjlkjnlsdnlkdnf.
Actually, does it start tomorrow for you too? Do home school
kids have to follow the normal schedule or is it just kind of a free
for all?*

*Anyways, everyone's all excited about it. My parents are fricking
estatic and keep dropping these incredibly not subtle hints about
how great it'll be to have a "fresh start".*

*Here's the deal, Sadie. Growing up's a trap. You get a grade older
and suddenly everyone decides that you're going to become this
brand-new, better person than you were the day before. You
know what though? No one bothered asking if I actually want to
be brand new.*

*When adults say "mature" they really just mean quiet and like
yeah, I get sometimes I'm a bit louder than I probably should be,
but that's a whole hell of a lot better than being too quiet, you
know? Unless high school magically stops the rest of the world
from being annoying, I'm not going to stop calling it out. The
maturity thing's a lie. I think maybe I'm actually too mature
sometimes and that freaks out the adults around me.*

It's probably like, against the rules of teen girl-dom to say this, but

47

I like this me. I'm not going to trade her in for a better model just because she sometimes makes other people uncomfortable.

Sending you strength to get through another year of having to live with your teachers,
Skye

From: Sadie
To: Skye

I like this you too. I think she's the perfect volume.

From: Skye
To: Sadie

Sdjndsfnlsdjsdklfdsfns way to ruin my whole angsty teen thing, Sadie.

From: Skye
To: Sadie

That was a joke. Please continue to shower me in compliments.

From: Skye
To: No one

I think maybe you're my favourite sound and I haven't even heard you talk yet. Is that weird?

Isaac offered to drive her home after school. She always offered.

Skye always said no.

She made sure her bag was packed right at the bell so that she could hop on her bike and rush down to the elementary school. Graduating had made the exchanges both easier and harder. It meant an extra stop now every time she wanted to leave or pick something up, but at least now if she got there quickly enough, there were no curious teachers on supervision duty who'd been trained to keep her away from the O'Brian fence.

She rode her bike all the way up the lawn and threw her bag to the ground. When she pulled aside the stone they used to hide the hole (smooth and perfect, Skye'd spent ages looking for it at the lake years earlier. She'd carved her initials onto the flat underside with her house key. Sadie'd written hers in pencil, as if that was somehow a lesser act of vandalism) she found the Tupperware container she'd left there the week before containing a tiny paper crane. Skye grinned, taking an identical container of homemade gingersnaps out from the side pocket of her bag and swapping the two. They rarely left each other physical letters anymore. Now that Sadie was less paranoid about emails, there wasn't really a point. They'd never get sick of Wednesday item swaps though.

Until the end of this year. Until Skye left. They never talked about what would come after that though.

Skye hopped back on her bike and rode to her second stop. She'd loitered. She didn't have time for loitering. There was a stack of textbooks in her bag just waiting to be pre-studied.

"Hey Mum!" She planted a quick kiss on her cheek as she ducked behind the bakery's counter.

Her mother scoffed slightly. She was the kind of person you'd look at and instantly call kind. Short stature and kind smile and thick arms perfect for hugging. That she always smelt slightly of cinnamon was just an added bonus. "Here to rob me again?" She teased.

Skye nodded, already heading towards the back. "We're going to Isaac's. It's tradition."

"There are leftovers on top of the fridge!" Her mother called after her. "Don't take anything new!"

"Got it!"

So, it was to the fridge then to the front then back to her bike then off to Isaac's. Like she'd done hundreds of times before. Like she'd hopefully only have to do a couple dozen more before leaving it all behind her.

She stuffed a cookie into her mouth, balanced the rest on her lap, and took off.

From: Sadie
To: Skye

I've been thinking a lot about hauntings, recently. I think it's the time of year. Did you know people originally dressed up on Halloween to ward of ghosts because they thought it was the night when the veil between the living and the dead was the thinnest? Isn't it weird that now we use it as an excuse to indulge in spooky things instead of trying to scare them off? There's something morbidly poetic about dressing as the very thing you fear.

Maybe we do it because our biggest fear is turning into that. Entering one side of the void and not being able to come back. Maybe instead of warding off the dead we now use Halloween to try and imagine them being here with us because now that we're no longer dropping like flies, there is nothing more terrifying than being forgotten.

Anyways, I'm not sure if we've established if you believe in ghosts yet, but I'd like to think you do. You seem open minded like that. And also like you'd want to believe in them just because they make everything a bit more exciting. I've attached a few of my favourite ghost stories if you wanted to look through them.

If you do believe in ghosts—or if you don't too, I guess. It's just a thought experiment—would you rather come back and be stuck in limbo for all of eternity or fade off into nothingness? Sometimes both seem equally horrifying.

Yours,
Sadie

From: Skye
To: Sadie

Can't believe you'd even ask if I'd be a ghost. Absolutely. I'd cause so much shit I'd become notorious. We could be like, ghost co-conspirators and haunt this entire fucking town until we scare everyone else away and then all that spooky limbo stuff won't even matter because we can't be damned or forgotten if we do it together, right?

I printed off your stories and scared the shit out of my friends last night, so thanks for helping me be a terror. They're appropriately intimidated by your knowledge of all things spooky.

P.S. I'm shoving an insane amount of Halloween candy into the hideout after school today. Make sure you get to it before your parents find it.

-   Skye

"She arrives!" Isaac announced, throwing open the door with flourish.

Skye rolled her eyes when she instantly went for the cookies. "Sometimes I feel like you only keep me around for the baked goods."

"Oh, that's absolutely why we keep inviting you." Isaac bit into a brownie. "Come on." She tilted her head, strings of dark brown hair falling into her eyes. Isaac kept her hair just far enough from shoulder length that no one asked questions. Her bangs were in a constant state of disarray, but she never let anyone else cut it. "Everyone's waiting. Kyle brought a girl and we haven't finished giving him shit yet."

Skye followed her.

Isaac's basement was Skye's single favourite place in town. It always smelt vaguely of must, but in the warm cozy way, not the kind that made you worry about asbestos. It was small and square and definitely not big enough to hold four mix-matched worn in couches, but the Abrahms' lack of literally any other furniture somehow made it feel cozier. Skye didn't detest all small things, just the ones that made her feel too big. Isaac's basement was a parallel universe where everything always fit just right.

The walls were plastered in posters and pictures. Half of them ironic (posters for children's shows and boybands graffitied in years of pencil and sharpy, random cut outs from the yearbook of kids that they barely knew but had decided to hate all the same) and half of them genuine. There were 'live, laugh, love' posters and declarations of how 'in this house, we listen to each other' sprinkled between random pictures of fish and a declaration of 'mancave rules'. Skye liked that one the most because only she and Isaac got to understand that it was put up with just as much irony as everything else. That one belonged to just the two of them.

As the only out girl in the group, it was somehow her unspoken duty to sit beside the very tense looking girl beside

Kyle. Skye took off her backpack and sat down on the cushion next to her.

"Hi," the girl said. She was blonde and quiet and soft and definitely a foreign presence in the basement. "I'm Hillary."

"Skye," said Skye.

Trevor hadn't shown up yet and everyone was talking amongst themselves while they waited, so Skye sat in awkward silence, daydreaming about all the more productive things she could be doing. She tried talking to Hillary a few times.

"Watch any good shows recently?"

"Not really."

"You in any clubs?"

"Loads."

Skye really wished she was at least interesting. People were constantly assuming that as the only obvious girl in a group of what they thought were all guys, she secretly detested all other women and was in love with at least two of her friends. Her being an out lesbian apparently didn't help dispel that last bit. If anything, that was also for attention. Skye tried her best to never dislike any other girls out of principle but sometimes, it was really, really hard to try and be friends with some of them.

Kyle, for his part, was too busy talking to Avan and Isaac to pay his date any attention. Skye would have to yell at him later. Sometimes it was painful seeing how inept at dating her friends were even though they had everything in the universe lined up to help them.

"Holy shit!" Trevor froze at the base of the stairs when he finally arrived. "There's a girl here."

"I'm a girl!" Skye rose her hand to correct him, more because Isaac couldn't than because she actually thought that the correction would do anything.

Because, like always, Trevor just rolled his eyes and followed with "yeah, but you don't count," and like always, she rolled her eyes back and pretended that it didn't bother her.

And if you asked anyone but Skye, it didn't. If you asked anyone but Skye, it was an honour.

She'd always hated that. That the goal for girls like her was to be "one of the guys" because she'd always known that it was a thinly veiled attempt to correct the fact that there weren't supposed to be "girls like her" at all. She didn't envy people like Isaac who got stuck with an assigned gender that didn't fit them, but she also wished that people didn't make it so obvious that they thought that hers didn't fit her. Skye was not one of the boys. She was a girl who liked girls and a girl who could be loud or violent or crude, but she was still a girl. Next to people like Hillary though, it was hard to remind herself of that sometimes. Sometimes, Skye thought she was a different species entirely.

(Maybe a fairy, though she didn't know about any of that yet)

Isaac jumped up. "Everyone got their papers?"

"Papers?" Hillary asked.

She resisted the urge to roll her eyes. Kyle hadn't prepared the poor thing at all.

"Course outlines," she explained. "We're burning them."

"Why?"

There had been a reason, at some point. Something poetically snarky that Isaac had probably come up with back in ninth grade. But by then, the honest answer was just "because we can."

They filed up the stairs one at a time and for a moment, Skye considered missing them in a year.

Kyle, with his never-ending slew of love interests, looking like he'd stepped straight out of some movie where the high school quarterback inevitably gets the girl. Who'd call Skye a month from now when things inevitably fell apart with Hillary when he fell faster than she did, let her let him win at Mario Kart in her basement for hours, and then swear her to secrecy and never let her bring up Hillary again.

Avan whose presence as the only straight guy in the entire twelfth grade drama class meant he was extremely hot to an extremely niche group of the school who still blushed when anyone said anything remotely nice to him and made them all swear to never go to any of his performances (the school recorded them and Skye was pretty sure they'd all bought a DVD to watch him after the fact at least once, but it was a betrayal so secret that they didn't even tell each other).

Trevor who was in three separate D&D campaigns a week but somehow still found time for them in between preparing for some non-existent comic trivia tournament he would school the entire planet on who offered to help her design a character no matter how many times she told him that she was too busy to commit to anything more than one shots. Who'd spent years inviting her to everything just to let her turn him down.

And Isaac, their fearless leader who kidnapped them all from whatever social cliques they would have been destined to be a part of in any other universe. Who'd declared that orientation week groups had to stick together for life and then held them all to thar. Who'd come out to Skye as gay then bi then trans then straight and helped research all the million little micro labels Skye'd worked her way through in ninth grade before landing back on lesbian. Isaac who understood all of them in some unperceivable Isaac way that made her impossible not to be friends with.

Some high school friends stayed close after graduating, but Skye already knew that they wouldn't. They had nothing in common but a shared animosity for the shit little town they'd grown up in and they were all going to run away from it the first moment that they could. But somehow, that made her love them more. Isaac was going to Toronto with her and she was sure that she'd try to keep in contact with everyone else, but Skye knew they'd eventually stop talking.

She'd be fine with that. Getting out was worth that. She just hadn't finished becoming fine with it yet.

They lit Isaac's bonfire and Skye gave Hillary half of her papers because someone had to, and they all whooped and cheered as they went up in flames. When Isaac got out the marshmallows, Hillary mentioned something about "ink-poisoning" and Skye already knew that she wouldn't last. Kyle and them were a package deal and other people rarely worked with that. She handed her some of the remaining cookies so she'd at least have something to do while the rest of them feasted on burnt sugar.

"Do you have more?" Hillary pointed to the Tupperware container at side of her bag. "Not that you have to share, obviously, they're just really—"

Skye's ears went pink. Trevor whistled.

"What?" Hillary's forehead creased. "What did I—"

"It's from her girlfriend," Kyle leaned in to stage whisper.

"Oh!" Hillary blushed. "I didn't realize—"

"She's not my girlfriend." Skye pulled out the container because if everyone was already looking at it, she didn't see a point in keeping it hidden. "We're just friends."

"Sure," someone sang. It could have been one of them or all of them. The effect was the same.

"Her parents are total freaks," Skye explained, carefully pulling out the paper crane. "Always putting her on random diets and shit. I sneak her stuff and she trades me for it."

Hillary frowned. "She trades you origami?"

"Exactly." Skye nodded. She was trying very hard to like Hillary for Kyle's sake, but she didn't see how she was supposed to put up with someone who turned up their nose at handcrafted birds.

"It's the O'Brian girl," Kyle whispered.

Skye punched his shoulder.

"What!" He laughed. "It is! It's not like it's a secret."

Hillary was really staring at her now.

"The one from middle school?"

"She existed past middle school."

"Right, but... the one we wrote to?"

Skye gritted her teeth as she nodded.

"Geez!" Hillary laughed. "I thought she was fake or dead or something."

"We have a running bet going that she's imaginary," Kyle informed her, plucking the crane out of her palm.

Skye reached (to hit him again or grab it back, she wasn't sure) but he got up to dodge and she decided that it wasn't worth abandoning her marshmallow.

"She's real," she said. "Her name's Sadie."

"Why can't she leave the house?"

Skye shrugged. "I don't know."

"You don't—"

"Holy shit!" Kyle exclaimed.

Skye's head snapped to him and the now unfolded piece of paper. She jumped to her feet, abandoning her stick on the lawn. Apparently, if you folded a thousand cranes, you got a wish. Skye knew that that wasn't true and that Sadie knew that wasn't true, but she still didn't want to deal with the hypothetic repercussions of one being unfolded. "What did you—"

"Do you have O'Brian girl's number?"

"No, we email. She—"

He flipped the paper around, grinning. "You do now."

Skye lunged, but he was a student athlete and she was a student nothing so when he sprinted off with it, she didn't stand a chance.

"Let's all talk to her!" he said.

"I'll kill you."

"It'll be fun!"

He ran and she ran and she knew that she had no hope of ever catching up to him but then Isaac stood up, said "let me see", and they both miraculously listened.

She looked at Skye. "Are we calling her?"

Skye rolled her eyes. "Sure, why not?"

Her heart thudded with a hundred "why not"s, but none of them were strong enough to counteract the millions of "of course"s that needed to try the number as soon as possible.

Isaac pulled out her phone to dial. It rang and rang and rang and Skye quickly realized that this was an awful idea, but then her biggest hope and fear came to be simultaneously. Someone picked up.

Everyone was gesturing wildly at her, so she said, "hello?"

But there was no reply.

She repeated it, louder this time. "Hello?"

Still nothing.

"Hey!" Trevor leaned over the phone. "Mystery girl? You there?"

They all tried, but one by one, they were each met with static. Eventually, the line went dead. They all leaned over the phone as if Sadie would finally say something even though she had no way to anymore. Something about her had always seemed a bit supernatural, so it didn't feel entirely outside of the realm of possibilities.

Then, Kyle said "told you she was fake", Skye rolled her eyes and punched his shoulder, and things went back to normal.

Maybe it was a prank. Or a number left on a piece of paper that she was never supposed to open. Whatever it had been, she waited until everyone was distracted listening to Avan tell a story about some teacher he'd decided that they should all hate before slipping the square of paper into her pocket.

To: Sadie
From: Skye

I got kicked off debate today. I'm honestly surprised I lasted the month.

It's not even really a big deal. I didn't want to join in the first place, I only did it so my parents would stop freaking out and because some overachieving guidance counsellor told them that academic arguing would be a "more healthy outlet" for me after I got in an argument with a history teacher for teaching history wrong as if I was in any way the problem there.

Anyways, we were doing the whole "trans bathroom debate" which is bullshit anyways but it felt especially bullshitty and targeting because I'm the only out queer person in the club. I know you haven't had to experience the particular brand of covert homophobia that is living in this shithole, Sadie, but there are so few out people here that if you're out as any kind of queer, you become the de facto spokesperson for all of it.

I obviously just repeated my pro trans people doing whatever the hell they want rant twice regardless of whatever side they put me on which was apparently unacceptable because we're supposed to be able to "argue both sides" but that implies that there actually is any other valid side in that argument which there isn't which is exactly why it shouldn't be up for debate at all, let alone the topic of a fucking debate club but apparently democracy's dead because if you try to inform the law teacher in charge of the club that he's enabling the transphobic assholes who suggested the topic you get kicked out. My parents already paid the tournament fee so I'm sure they'll be pissed about that but I'm gonna start working at the bakery this summer anyways so I'll just pay them back.

I know it's just a few years and I should let things go or whatever, but if everyone's decided I'm their queer spokesperson I'm sure as fuck going to be loud about it. I can't wait until graduation. Then it'll just be me, Isaac, a shitton of student debt, and an overpriced basement apartment in Toronto. Still probably homophobic as shit, but at least there'll be enough other queer people there that I'll be able to walk down the street without some random stranger sharing their opinions on my sexuality. Bare minimum, but still.

Anyways, I know staying in debate would have probably worked better for the "get good grades, get accepted at UofT, get out" plan, but I've been reading up on clubs and they're a lot less important in STEM programs unless you want like, giant scholarships and I should probably have enough saved up by then that I'll survive. If you have any other club suggestions though, I'm all ears.

P.S. You'd kick ass at debate, by the way. You're infinitely better at keeping your cool than me and you actually research things like, voluntarily. If they let home school kids compete, you should look into it.

- *Skye*

From: Sadie
To: Skye

:(sorry people suck. It's their loss, I'm sure your parents won't mind. I wouldn't have wanted to debate that either.

Anyways, would you rather have elephant ears or dragonfly eyes?

From: Skye
To: No one

Okay but like, because you're queer and personally invested or because it's objectively a shitty stance?

It'd be really helpful if you stopped responding to all my very gay emails without letting me know if you relate.

From: Skye
To: Sadie

Eyes. Obviously.

Skye didn't realize that she hadn't told anyone about her plan until Isaac texted her hours later while she was lying awake, trying to trick her body into sleeping.

Isaac: *Ominous plan isn't a go then?*

It was. It would be. But getting a possible phone number from the girl you'd been obsessing over for a decade would make it pretty difficult for anyone to focus on pretty much anything else. The sentiment was apparently shared, because Isaac immediately sent a follow up message.

Isaac: *Has she picked up yet?*

Not "have you called her again?" like Avan had sent before she'd even finished biking home or the "you should call her again" she'd gotten from Kyle during dinner or even the three unanswered "call her." texts from Trevor. Because Isaac would always know her best, whether that was because they were united in queerdom or femininity or secrecy or some indescribable link that Isaac had been certain existed from that first day of ninth grade. Of course she would know that Skye had already tried calling again.

She did once more while she lied there, just to see what would happen. Like every call except the first, it rang all the way through. A non-descript, robotic answering machine clicked on, and Skye quickly hung up the phone.

She switched back to her texts.

Skye: *No*

Isaac: *To which?*

Skye: *Both. Ominous plan still on*

Isaac: *I'll rally the troops again for tomorrow then.*

She didn't ask about Sadie again. Skye knew that she wanted to, but she didn't.

Skye groaned, rolling over to face her ceiling. She told herself that it was no big deal. Sadie was a game. A mystery she kept telling herself that she was trying to solve even though she'd given up on that years ago. They still had emails and letters which was probably better in the long run anyway. She'd be leaving in a few months and Sadie would be staying forever, so she absolutely didn't need to get addicted to the sound of her voice.

She'd seen her a few times too, to ease her friends' constant insistence that she was being catfished by some 50-year-old creep. Brief, meticulously timed waves through windows before curtains abruptly fell back into place. Never long enough to remember anything about her, but still the realest thing that she'd let herself think she'd be able to get.

There was no reason to be excited about a maybe number. She should have ignored it. She couldn't.

She pulled her computer onto the bed and waited in the darkness for it to power on.

From: Skye
To: Sadie

Hey!
There was a number on the crane you left. Was I supposed to call it?

She powered both her phone and computer all the way down so she wouldn't be able to check them again. She wouldn't know that she'd gotten an instant reply until the next morning.

From: Sadie
To: Skye

Yes.

From: Sadie
To: Skye

I heard my parents talking about you today. As far as they know, it's been years since you had anything to do with any of us and they still randomly bring you up just to complain. I think they're almost as obsessed with you as I am—don't worry, that was a very, very, liberal almost.

It still got me thinking though. You had all these theories about what I was, right? Which one are you most disappointed wasn't true?

My personal favourite would have to be spy. That'd be far more exciting.

From: Skye
To: Sadie

No.

From: Sadie
To: Skye

???

From: Skye
To: Sadie

Can't answer because I'm not disappointed. You turned out to be better than any spy or ghost or alien or robot every could've been.

From: Skye
To: Sadie

Show that last email to anyone and the ghost theory'll come true early though.

From: Skye
To: Sadie

Just kidding. (About the murder implication, not not wanting you to show anyone)

From: Sadie
To: Skye

:)

"Is this about the O'Brian girl?"

Skye rolled her eyes, pushing Trevor's legs off of the coffee table so she could squeeze past him to sit beside Hillary. She'd apparently decided that she wasn't done with them yet. She must have really liked Kyle.

"Sadie," Skye corrected. They would always call her "the O'Brian girl" and she would always correct them even though she knew that it would change nothing. It was just how they worked. "And no, it's not."

She'd called Sadie again before class and then again on her bike ride over to Isaac's, but all it had earned her was a *sorry, we'll try again later*, text.

At least now she knew that the number actually belonged to someone.

"This," Skye dramatically revealed. "Is about to make us all look more well rounded on uni aps."

"You said that barely mattered," Kyle reminded her.

Skye shrugged. "It probably doesn't. But being in a club has to look good on personal essays, right?"

"We're all in some already," Trevor (extremely unhelpfully) pointed out.

"Well, I'm not. And you all love me so you're going to join whichever one I start."

He rolled his eyes. "What kind of club?"

"Whatever one'll sound the best to whatever new teachers we have this year. We need someone untainted."

Kyle leaned towards Hillary. "That's code for someone who doesn't know how annoying she is yet."

Skye threw a cookie at his head. He caught it and chewed smugly.

"Ms. Rivera's new," Isaac volunteered. "She's in the English department."

"Perfect." Skye clapped. "We'll start a writing club or book club or something."

Skye didn't have much of a personal investment in the literary arts, but she already knew who to ask for help. It would take her months to realize that there were half a dozen new teachers at the school that year that Isaac would have been more likely to think of before Ms. Rivera. She was truly an excellent wingwoman.

"Everyone'll join, be on their best behavior for a few months, and then boom! Glowing recommendation letter and I become a doctor or some shit and let you all visit one of my several beach houses."

She didn't miss Hillary's frown at that.

"What?" Skye asked. "Have something against beaches?"

"No, I—" her eyes darted to Kyle, but he just stared back at her. "It's just... you need more than a few nice words to get into something that'll work for pre-med. Don't you think you should maybe—"

"Skye's the smart one," Isaac cut her off, because she was the nice one.

The rest of the group nodded their heads in agreement.

Hillary stared at Kyle again, but he just shrugged. "Yeah, Skye's the smart one. I mean, the bar isn't exactly high, but..."

"Oh," Hillary blushed. "I just thought... it didn't seem like... forget it."

Skye's entire body went hot. Isaac must have noticed the temperature change because her hand was suddenly wrapped around her arm. Skye had a penchant for attacking things when she overheated. "What the fuck does that mean?"

"Nothing, I just figured..." Hillary winced. "I mean, you don't exactly seem like the studious type, Skye."

She stared. Because to her, Hillary didn't *seem* like anything. Because before yesterday, Hillary hadn't even crossed her mind. Isaac's grip went tight on her arm, but she didn't have to worry. Skye wasn't planning on staining her cushions so instead, she went perfectly still.

Everyone watched Isaac because she was in charge of everything, but it was Kyle who spoke first.

"Get out."

Hillary blinked. "I—what?"

"You're leaving. Get out."

"You can't just—"

"We'll talk upstairs."

Kyle stormed off, Hillary followed, and the rest of them waited in tense silence. When he returned, he was all smiles and nonchalance and decidedly alone. He flopped back onto the couch and threw an arm around Skye's shoulders.

"So," he asked. "When are we recruiting this poor English teacher?"

Skye gnawed at her lip. "Sorry. You didn't have to—"

"No, fuck that. We don't date assholes. English teacher. When."

"As soon as possible?"

Isaac nodded. "I'll help track her down spare period tomorrow."

"Thanks, I—" Skye jumped off the cushion.

Her phone was ringing.

From: Sadie
To: Skye

If you could go anywhere in the world, where would you go?

From: Skye
To: Sadie

With you?

From: Sadie
To: Skye

Sure. Hypothetically, obviously.

From: Skye
To: Sadie

Everywhere.

Skye couldn't remember the last time her phone had rung. She kept it on silent most of the time since no one called anymore anyway, but there it was, ringing. She fumbled to pull it out of her pocket.

"Is it her?" Avan asked.

Four heads leaned towards her as she stared bug-eyed at the screen.

"I need to—" Her palms suddenly felt incredibly hot. She was sure she'd drop the phone. "I should—"

"Right." Isaac jumped up. "Everyone upstairs. Now."

"But—" Trevor started.

"Upstairs!"

They all muttered in protest but complied.

"Good luck with your phone sex!" Trevor called as they went.

That definitely didn't help with the hand shaking.

She picked up the call.

"I... hello?"

"Hello," the voice on the other side of the phone said. Skye tried to match it with how she was pretty sure Sadie looked, but it was slightly higher than the voice she'd been using in her head had been. She didn't realize that she'd given her a voice in her head at all until confronted with how poorly they matched. "May I ask whom I'm speaking to?"

It would have been a jarring conversation starter if Skye wasn't already battling burning hands and a thundering heart and reframing her entire mental image of her favourite made-up voice. "Skye," she said. "Umm... Eaton."

"Oh, good! It's Sadie."

She was in her contacts so Skye already knew that, but her body went hot all over again at the confirmation.

"Hi," she said.

"Hi."

"Hi."

"Hi."

"Hi."

Skye laughed.

"Sorry," Sadie said. "I'm umm... not really good at this."

"I'm being equally awkward, Sade." *Sade.* What she'd imagined herself calling her a million times but had figured she never would. Nicknames were a vital part of year long friendships, but it felt weird dropping one over email. She caught it slip out and pressed a fist to her knee. "You're fine."

"Okay," she breathed into the phone. Or maybe that was how she laughed. Skye didn't know yet. "Sorry," she said again. "This is weird."

"Good weird?"

"I hope so."

They were both quiet.

"I tried calling yesterday," Skye said. *And this morning and like thirty minutes ago* felt too clingy to add.

"Right. Yes. Sorry, I was nervous."

Skye sprawled herself out on the couch and stared at the ceiling. Sometimes her thoughts were easier to organize when she was horizontal. "So," she said. "You have a phone now?"

"Yes. I'm a year away from graduating so..."

"Cool. That's good. Now I can annoy you all the time."

"I don't want you to do that."

Skye laughed. "Then I'll stick to some of the time."

"If I don't pick up it's not... I might get nervous. Again. Keep calling though."

Skye wondered, not for the first time, not even for the hundredth, what Sadie was refusing to tell her. If there really was some mystery illness keeping her from leaving the house or even just picking up the phone that she was hiding.

"Okay," she whispered instead of asking. Asking never got her anywhere. "That's good to know."

"How was your day?" Sadie asked. "What are you doing right now?"

"Holding Isaac's basement hostage to talk to you."

"Oh. If you need to go, I can—"

"No! They can wait. I get to talk to them all the time. You're more interesting."

There was a dull thud on her side of the line. "Sadie?" Skye checked. "Everything okay?"

"Yes!" She called. "I just dropped something."

"I'm thinking of starting a writing club," Skye said. "Or reading club. We didn't actually figure that part out yet. You want in?"

"I don't go to your school."

"You can be our off-campus advisor. It'll be good practice."

Sadie was going to be an author. It was one of the first things Skye had learned about her and she'd never wavered once on it. It was as much a part of her as other people's eye colours were a part of them.

"Okay," she said. Or called. Her voice suddenly sounded less clear. "You should probably go, right? Before your friends get back?"

"They can wait. I—"

"I think you'd better go."

Skye's heart sank. "Oh. Right."

Without any fanfare or even a goodbye, the line clicked off.

From: Sadie
To: Skye

If you could have dinner with one person, dead or alive, who would it be?

From: Skye
To: Sadie

See, now I feel like you're just trying to get me to compliment you. You already know my answer.

From: Sadie
To: Skye

I was. You caught me.

The phone rang again before she'd even left the couch.

"Hello?"

"Call me again, alright? When you have more time? I'd really..." She paused. "I really, really, like talking to you."

Skye smiled. "I really, really, like talking to you too."

The phone went silent again. Skye kicked her feet in the air, though she'd never admit that to anyone.

From: Sadie
To: Skye

My answer was the same, by the way.

From: Skye
To: Sadie

Yeah, obviously.

"Hello." She listened to her voice through earbuds, though there was no reason to use them in her own bedroom. She felt closer that way, with the pressure in her ears. "Sadie O'Brian speaking."

Skye smiled, shifting down further in her comforter. "Hi, Sadie O'Brian."

It was supposed to be a joke. It was an attempt at lightly poking fun at her. But then she responded with "hello Skye Eaton," and everything suddenly felt extremely serious.

Skye's breath caught in her throat.

"Skye?"

"Still here," she said.

Skye did get nervous (despite what other people liked to believe). She got nervous when she had to talk with an adult one on one and when the cashier at Macdonald's with the cool earrings asked what she wanted to order. She got nervous before tests and during tests and after tests and when teachers announced partner projects. She was nervous about her future and nervous about her present and even nervous about what parts of her past would inevitably come back to haunt her. But she had never been as obviously, painfully nervous as that second first conversation with Sadie. Skye was not immune to nervousness (despite what other people like to believe). But even if she had been, even if she was, Sadie O'Brian was her kryptonite.

She had the biggest crush of her life on a girl she'd never even get to look at properly.

"How was your day?" Sadie asked. "How are your friends?"

"Good. Or, you know, annoying, but in a good way. What about you?"

"Good."

Skye could feel the conversation grinding to a halt. She needed to keep her on the line. "How's the writing going? What are you working on right now?"

Sadie was always working on something, Skye secretly thought that that was why she never got anything finished. She'd send paragraphs and paragraphs of plot outlines one day then already be on to the next thing the next. They were retellings, mostly. Sometimes contemporary where the prince and princess meet at a coffee shop or sometimes fantasy where the meet-cute instead happened in a forest with knives at each other's throats, but they were always retellings. Of what, Skye was never sure until she inevitably gave up guessing and Sadie sent her the link to whatever source material she'd used. Half the time the plot would seem so Beauty and the Beast-esque that she was certain she'd gotten it right. It was never Beauty and the Beast. It turned out a lot of fairy tales were basically just Beauty and the Beast in different fonts. Skye wasn't sure what that said about their ancestors, but she knew it probably wasn't good.

Skye believed that Sadie was going to become a famous author because Sadie believed that Sadie was going to become a famous author but secretly, she was always looking for ways to gently tell her that she'd have to change strategies. Skye didn't have much time for reading, but you didn't have to be obsessed with books to know that retellings didn't tend to sell until they were of the kinds of stories popular enough to catch Disney's attention. The general public was probably never going to be interested in girls whose fathers hacked off their hands or fish who turned wives into emperors. It would catch Skye's (particularly the ones that involved limb-chopping) but she knew a lot of that probably had to do with the girl telling her about them.

They were all also straight, even when they didn't have to be. Beans and straw turned to men and women just to make each retelling a bit more heteronormative. So, there was that.

Sadie talked. Skye knew she would, the girl lived for telling other people stories. It wasn't until she started describing the next plot she'd probably abandon that Skye realized that she'd never heard her talk before, not really. Her voice picked up speed and got higher as she went, as if the story would escape her if she didn't get to the ending in time. She spoke the way Skye thought, all half-finished sentences that decided to become something else entirely partway through and thoughts interrupted by her own commentary on them and a thousand new ideas a second. Skye wondered if this was how it worked when she emailed her plots too. If she sat down knowing where she was planning on ending up and then changed things completely while she typed. Sadie didn't take a single audible breath for a full fifteen minutes so it would have been impossible for Skye to add anything even if she came up with something worth contributing, but somehow it felt almost collaborative. Skye leaned against her pillow, let her eyes fall shut, and listened.

"Skye?" Sadie's voice abruptly slowed down again.

Skye smiled. "Still here."

"Sorry if that was too much. You could stop me if I ever—"

"Are you kidding me? And let you leave me on a cliff-hanger? I'd go insane."

Sadie was quiet.

"You should help with it," Skye said. "That reading club or writing club or whatever it is I'm starting. You'd be good at that."

"I can't just come to your school."

"You can do this though, right? I can just like... put you on speaker."

She was quiet again. Skye's pulse hammered in her ears. "Okay."

Skye fist-pumped the air so aggressively that the rest of her body was pulled up with it. "Awesome! I'll you know, actually make sure we're allowed to run it then let you know, okay? Talk again tomorrow?"

"Tomorrow," Sadie echoed, then hung up the phone without saying goodbye. It didn't feel like an ending though, Skye was pretty sure it was the promise of a beginning.

From: Skye
To: No one

*I think you're maybe the only person in the world who makes me
feel like me and sometimes that's fucking unbearable because
you're also the only person in the world I know I'm never going to
be able to have an actual conversation with and I can't even ask
why without feeling like an asshole.*

*I hope you're okay. I wish I was naive enough to believe that
you're genuinely okay.*

*Honestly though, if you were, if we did meet properly, we
wouldn't have been friends, Sadie. I'm kind of a dick? Like, less
so now, I hope, but I was definitely a dick in elementary school so
I'm kind of glad we never got the chance to talk in person because
you wouldn't have been able to stand me. Which makes me feel
like shit because you're probably fucking dying or something and
I'm over here being grateful that you can't leave your house.*

*Like, Isaac's great and wonderful and practically a saint but she's
just too nice to hate me and kept giving me second chances until I
stopped fucking it up and I can't even be entirely honest with her
like I can with you.*

What the fuck's wrong with me?

Isaac was waiting at Skye's locker when she got to school the next morning.

"How's your girlfriend doing?"

Skye rolled her eyes, shouldering past her to enter her combination. "How are you only ever early for things when it's to annoy me?"

"You're deflecting."

"No," Skye started pulling her binders out of her bag a bit more aggressively than normal. "You asked a nonsense question, so I didn't answer it. I don't have a girlfriend."

Isaac just stared at her, eyebrows raised.

"What! I don't! I have a girl who's my friend. That's different."

"How long did you spend talking to her last night?"

"Only like, half an hour."

"And how long did you spend hovering near your phone not getting any work done in case she called?"

She'd already dropped off everything she needed, but Skye kept her focus on the top shelf of her locker as she mumbled something unintelligible.

Isaac sighed, slamming the locker shut. "I'm sorry, what was that?"

"Like... two hours." Skye admitted. "And a half. But she's just a friend. I'm allowed to have other friends, you know."

"If I asked you to spend three hours on me on a school night, you'd—"

"I would."

Her eyes narrowed. "Okay, fine, but you'd give me like, so much shit about it after. Endless shit. And not only am I absolutely sure you're not even going to complain a bit to her about it, you're probably going to waste three hours again tonight then be stressed about it all day tomorrow."

Skye chewed on her lip. "She's straight."

"Sure," Isaac sang. She'd known Skye long enough to lean away when she lunged at her. "Come," she spun away from her before she could properly strategize her next attack. "We have a teacher to trick."

The thing about Isaac (one of Skye's most and least favourite things about Isaac) was that she didn't actually have to trick anyone into anything. People seemed to like her just for existing. It was why they both knew that she would have to be the one to summon Ms. Rivera out of the English office without either girl having to officially propose the idea. Skye waited in the hall as Isaac remerged with a tall, pant-suited woman.

"This is Skye," she introduced them. "Skye, Ms. Rivera."

Skye knew that it was her cue to say something, but she pursed her lips shut and kept her focus on Isaac. She couldn't fuck everything up if she didn't even talk.

"Skye's the one who'd actually be running the club," Isaac elaborated. "I'm just her assistant."

"I really like writing." Skye blurted. Then remembered that they still hadn't decided what kind of English club it was. "And umm... reading."

Skye knew she wasn't just imagining Ms. Rivera deflate a little. Even knowing nothing about them, English teachers always loved people like Isaac. There was a big difference between girls they knew were girls taking on a leadership role and girls they thought were boys who didn't seem like massive douchebags showing literally any interest in their classes.

"We might actually co-run it," Skye added, earning her a subtly elbow to the ribs. "Haven't ironed everything out yet."

Ms. Rivera's smile returned. "That sounds wonderful! We'll just have to work out schedules and check and make sure no one else was planning on running anything similar, but then I think we're good to go. Wait here for a moment?" She popped back into the office, leaving them alone in the hall.

Isaac glared. "I don't have time to—"

"I know," Skye stopped her. "We'll just look more organized with two people. I'll do everything, I swear. It's not like anyone'll actually join. And Sadie said she'd help too, so—"

The door reopened and Skye froze.

"Step in for a moment?" Ms. Rivera offered.

Skye waited for Isaac to walk in first. As a rule, she never spent any more time around teachers than she had to.

"This is Mr. Kelter," Ms. Rivera led them to the back of the room. "He actually already runs creative writing on Wednesdays and a book club on Fridays! They're always looking for new members if—"

"No," Skye said.

Isaac pinched her side. She pinched back. She knew she was blowing things, but there was no way Mr. Kelter would ever write anything remotely nice about Skye, no matter how much ass kissing she did. She'd had him for both ninth and tenth grade English, before Skye had learned that it was best to stay quiet when you didn't agree with a teacher's "literary interpretations".

"Sorry," Skye tried to cover. "We just... we wanted to focus on handpicked material."

Ms. Rivera frowned. "I'm not sure we'd have enough student interest for two book clubs."

"That's—"

"Absolutely fine," Isaac stopped her, grabbing her arm. "Maybe we'll just join your club, Mr. Kelter." Her eyebrows shot up in mock alarm that only Skye was able to recognize. "Shoot! Sadie'll be really disappointed though, huh?"

Skye just blinked.

"If you had another friend who wanted to join, she's always welcome," Mr. Kelter said.

Isaac shook her head. "Sadie doesn't technically go to school here. That's partially why we wanted to start our own club, right, Skye? So she could join virtually?"

It took Mr. Kelter's eyes widening for Skye to realize what she was doing. Everyone knew everyone in town. Despite the

O'Brian's best efforts, Sadie was practically a local celebrity by that point.

"Sadie O'Brian?" The English teacher confirmed.

Skye nodded. "Yeah, she was really looking forward to it. But..."

"If she wanted to videocall in, I'm sure we could—"

Skye tried her best to look forlorn as she clicked her tongue. "Sadie's really particular about books. That's why we wanted to start a club centred around the ones she liked so we could all talk about them together. We were planning on having her be like, an honorary co-founder or whatever but..." Skye trailed off. She'd learned long ago that adults loved being able to finish her sentences for her.

"Who's—" Ms. Rivera started to ask.

The bell rang. "We'll see what we can do," Mr. Kelter said. "We'll be in touch."

Ms. Rivera emailed Isaac before lunch, giving her the go ahead.

"Sadie'll do it, right?" Isaac confirmed. "Because this is all definitely extremely Sadie-contingent right now."

"She said she would." Skye shrugged. Before, that had sounded exciting. An excuse to talk to her more. Now it was... less that. "She doesn't find out that we made it sound like it was for her though, alright?"

"Yeah, sure."

Skye frowned. Isaac was supposed to be the moral one. She didn't know why she seemed so much more comfortable with it than Skye felt. "Doesn't this feel kind of gross? Playing the 'sad chronically ill shut in' card when we know Sadie's not sick?"

Isaac didn't respond. Skye watched her tongue press against her cheek.

"She's fine," Skye reiterated. "She's just... I don't know, anxious about leaving the house or something. She's fine."

"Okay." She nodded. "I hope so too. But even if she's not, you're friends, right? She knows how much uni means to you. I'm sure she'd want to help."

Skye nodded. "Right, yeah."

From: Sadie
To: Skye

If you got a million dollars to stay on a deserted island for a year and could only bring one person and three things, what would you choose?

From: Skye
To: Sadie

You, obviously. And a phone, cell tower, and raft.

My turn. What's your type?

From: Sadie
To: Skye

I'm pretty sure those are cheating answers. I'd do a dog (for hunting, not eating), seeds, and a shovel. And you.

From: Skye
To: Sadie

Oh my god, I'm so sorry, I just saw that last email. My friends must have taken my phone and added that last question on to the end. You don't have to answer it.

From: Sadie
To: Skye

Oh, okay. No problem.

"Would you rather have feet for hands or hands for feet?"

Skye was staring at her bedroom ceiling again, phone pressed against her shoulder.

"Hands for feet, obviously. Extra opposable thumbs. What about you?"

There was silence on the other end of the line. Skye rolled her eyes. "What are you looking up?"

Silence for a few more seconds then, "if wrists are strong enough to support body weight for long periods of time without causing any damage."

"Can they?"

"Not sure. It doesn't look like anyone else has looked it up yet."

"I guess no one else came across the same Would You Rather list."

"It seems like it."

Skye bit down on her lip. That was one of the things she was quickly realizing didn't come across properly over email. She'd always known that Sadie responded to her being stupid or sarcastic with deadpan, but her tone stayed so serious over the phone that she sometimes wasn't sure if that was intentional. She'd decided that someone not laughing at your joke was infinitely better than someone laughing at something that wasn't supposed to be one, so she tried her best to match Sadie's tone.

"You've been researching all of these, haven't you?" Skye accused. "For years!"

"Possibly. It's harder to do over the phone."

"And to think, I thought you were just full of really smart, insightful answers."

"I am. They're just also research-informed."

Skye smiled.

"Do you still like me?" Sadie checked. "Now that you know I'm not actually—"

"Don't be stupid, weird knowledge on the strength of human body parts isn't a friendship requirement."

"Okay, good." And "I still like you even now that I know you don't think through your answers enough."

That time, Skye did laugh. "Thanks for letting me know." She made herself sit up. "We're starting that club on Tuesday? The reading thing? We've decided it's a reading thing but we can talk about writing and stuff too, obviously."

"Oh. Okay."

"You still down to call in? It'll probably just be me and my friends and like, they're assholes, but extremely nice assholes. The best kind. I just have no idea how I'm supposed to pretend to talk about books for that long so if you wanted to rescue me..."

"Your school'd be alright with that?"

"Yeah, totally. Already ran it by them. They were actually going to make sure we got a room with a projector so you could videocall in but obviously I told them that wouldn't work so—"

"Why not?"

"I..." Skye frowned. "What?"

"I could videocall. That'd probably make more sense, right? So I could actually see who's talking?"

Skye's pulse picked up. "You're allowed to... won't your parents know?"

"I'm 17, Skye, I'm allowed on the internet. I videocall with internet friends all the time. And they pay my phone bill so they obviously—"

"Why haven't we done that!" Skye exclaimed.

"You never asked."

She flopped back again. "Then you're good to videocall in? On Tuesday?"

"Sure."

"Awesome. We'll mostly just pick books and stuff, but it should be chill. We can call after and talk over next steps."

"Sounds good."

"And Sadie?"

"Yeah?"

"This is me asking, okay? I'm getting tired of talking to the ceiling."

"I'll send you my Skype."

From: Sadie
To: Skye

I think I'm going to tell my parents about you.

From: Skye
To: Sadie

!!! Sadie!!! Abort! Run!

From: Sadie
To: Skye

Too late. Did it already. They seemed surprised, but fine.

From: Skye
To: Sadie

Sadie, they reported me to the school multiple times when I was only 10. There's no way it was fine.

From: Sadie
To: Skye

To be fair, you technically were harassing them. And you cracked the bird feeder.

They know now though, so we don't have to worry about being found out.

From: Skye
To: No one

Does that mean I can come see you in person now?

From: Skye
To: Sadie

Awesome

"Everyone's going to be on their best behavior, yeah?"

Skye summoned her friends to her locker right after the bell that Tuesday instead of meeting them in the classroom Ms. Rivera had reserved for them. She loved her friends, but she wasn't an idiot. This had to go perfectly, and they were just annoying enough to be the most likely source of imperfection.

Avan rolled his eyes. "Relax. We'll make sure your girlfriend knows you're wonderful."

"Okay, one," Skye pointed a finger at him. "Extremely not my girlfriend. Two, that's exactly not what we're doing. We're impressing Ms. Rivera, not Sadie."

Trevor whistled. "Damn, Skye. Ms. Rivera's—"

She spun to face him. "I'll actually kill you. Don't think I won't just because—"

He laughed, swatting down her arm. "Understood. No one's getting in between you and your imaginary girlfriend or the 30-year-old one."

"We're only talking about books," she looked them each in the eye, daring them to challenge her. "It'll be like a 30-minute meeting tops. It's virtually impossible to fuck up."

"Did Sadie get a pre-meeting lecture too?" Avan asked.

"No, because she actually knows how to go longer than five minutes without making a sex joke in front of a teacher."

All eyes turned to Isaac and she put up her arms in surrender. "Skye didn't even technically invite me here. I just like to feel included."

Skye nodded once. "This is going to be normal and proper and fine, okay?"

She waited to watch each of them nod back before starting off towards the classroom.

The original idea was to project Sadie's video feed onto the whiteboard, but Skye (with Isaac as a moderator to keep her from saying anything stupid before the first meeting even began) had managed to talk Ms. Rivera down to just keeping her on a computer unless a lot of students showed up.

She'd also made sure that that wouldn't happen. They hadn't run a single advertisement on the announcements or put up any posters and all of her friends had been sworn to secrecy. The last thing she needed was more moving parts to account for.

So (although she was acutely aware of Ms. Rivera watching their every move from her desk in the corner) she almost felt normal. She abandoned the whiteboard after it was officially ten minutes past the bell and no one else had shown up.

"We might as well all sit together then," she said. She'd only been alone at the board for a few minutes and could already tell that prolonged exposure would give her hives. "It doesn't seem like anyone else is showing up."

Sadie was supposed to log in via Ms. Rivera's laptop which felt excessively formal, but Skye'd already used up her one argument for the meeting. She should have insisted on meeting up with Sadie on videocall the night before, but every time she'd typed up the idea, she'd psyched herself out before hitting send. She didn't like knowing that the first time she saw her (really saw her, stolen glanced didn't count) would be the same moment all of her friends did. But then, Sadie's voice (because it was, even if it hadn't seemed like it that first time she'd heard it. Now she couldn't imagine it as anything else) was coming out from the speakers and Ms. Rivera was flipping her laptop around to put it on the end of the table, and she forgot that she'd been planning on being secretly frustrated.

Sadie didn't look like a ghost or alien or Russian spy. She wore a blue and pink knit sweater that reminded Skye of cotton candy before the undead. Her hair wasn't the white-ish blonde she'd remembered it being, it had turned so dark that it was almost brown. Her cheeks and forehead were covered in light freckles and she had pink eyeshadow above each of her green eyes. Sadie O'Brian was much too human for Skye to deal with in that moment.

"Hi," she said. Her voice sounded slightly more robotic than did over the phone. "I'm Sadie."

"Isaac." Isaac held up a hand, jabbing Skye in the side just as Avan stomped on her foot beneath the table.

Despite their forceful cueing, Skye couldn't remember how to talk until introductions had gone all the way around the table and back to her again.

"I'm Skye," she finally said.

The Sadie on the screen tilted her head to the side. "Yeah, I know."

Skye hoped that she was just imagining herself blushing.

Kyle squinted at the screen. "Are you sitting under a table right now?"

Sadie's eyes went wide. "Yeah, my laptop's awful at holding charge and the outlet's too far from the desk."

It was an awful lie, but Skye wasn't exactly looking for reasons to get her off the screen. She glanced at Ms. Rivera in the corner before clearing her throat and standing up.

"Anyways, if everyone's done with introductions, we can—"

"I'm sure chatting for a bit wouldn't hurt!" Ms. Rivera interjected. "We can all get to know each other a bit more while we wait for more people to show up."

Skye froze. She'd been looking for approval, not advice. The last thing she wanted was anyone getting to know each other. Or, more accurately, anyone getting to know pieces of her she hadn't shared with them yet.

Sadie spoke first, which was just about the most terrifying outcome possible. "Skye's told me a lot about all of you."

There was a collective snickering after Kyle said, "we've heard a lot about you too."

Skye made a mental note to yell at all of them about it later.

"Which of us is her favourite?" Trevor asked.

Skye didn't even get to finish rolling her eyes before Sadie said, "Isaac."

That earned a lot more than snickering.

"Sadie!" She exclaimed. "Not cool! That was confidential."

"Oh," she blushed. "Sorry."

"Don't worry, we already knew," Avan saved her. "They're obsessed with each other. It's very heterophobic."

"What about you?" Trevor leaned towards the screen. "Do you like—"

"Trevor." Skye glared at him. "Stop it. We're here to talk about books." She cleared her throat again, getting back up to try and regain control. "Unlike other book clubs, we at the Student Led Book Club want to focus on books that capture the wants and interests of actual students so we wanted to use this first meeting to go around and get book suggestions that we'll put into a random draw."

It was supposed to be the easy part. She'd given each of her friends a carefully curated list of slightly smart yet non-academic sounding books to memorize and pretend to suggest and they went through the first round of suggestions without a hitch. When they got back to Sadie though, none of them could hear you.

"Sadie," Skye said. "I think your mic's off."

She kept mouthing and gesturing for a few more seconds before Skye's phone buzzed.

"She says her mic must not be working. She'll just text me answers." She hoped she didn't make how relieved she was obvious. She wanted her friends to get to know Sadie because awesome people should get to know other awesome people, but she'd forgotten how much both groups knew about her. She needed more time to adjust.

Ms. Rivera pulled her and Isaac aside after the meeting to suggest ways to up attendance, she pretended to agree, then biked home as quickly as she could to call Sadie.

From: Sadie
To: Skye

Do you think they'd like me? Your friends?

From: Skye
To: Sadie

Anyone who wouldn't wouldn't be worth talking to.

"I think that went well," Sadie skipped introductions when she picked up the call. She was still hidden away under her table; Skye could see its underside brushing against the top of her head. She wondered if her parents actually did know about the videochatting.

Skye smiled. "Your mic's working again."

She blushed. "Was it obvious I was faking?"

"Absolutely not. I bought it and the rest of my friends are idiots so I'm sure no one was suspicious."

"They seem nice. There are just a lot of them."

Skye laughed. "Glad to hear I've tricked you into thinking I'm popular."

"You are though. They like you. I know it's childish, but I didn't want to say the wrong thing and—"

"Sadie," she stopped her. "Normally I think the wrong thing then just say it anyways. Your strategy's a lot smarter. It's fine, no one noticed."

She nodded. "I like your hair."

"I, umm—" Skye froze, reaching up to touch it. "Yours too. It's nice. Long."

"I pictured yours longer."

"I pictured yours shorter."

They stared at each other.

"The meeting went well," Skye tried to get things back on track. "Obviously it'll be harder when we actually have to talk about books because I doubt I'll get any of them to actually read anything, but it was a solid start. You might have to help me pull most of the weight once we get there though."

She grinned. "I'm extremely okay with monopolizing all the book talking stuff." Sadie hesitated. "If my mic goes out again or... I mean, not actually out, but if it seems like it does, you can't tell anyone."

Skye nodded. "I'm an excellent liar. Your secret's safe with me."

"I'm sorry I told them who you liked the most."

She laughed. "Trust me, they knew. They deserved to hear it. It'll help keep the rest of them in their place."

"I can avoid answering personal questions, if you want. I should have realized that was stupid."

"You're fine, my friends are just dicks. Tell them whatever."

Sadie frowned. "But you're worried about it, right? That's why you stopped that one—Trevor—when he tried to ask me something else?"

Skye's face went hot. "That wasn't... he wasn't going to ask something about being me. He was just being annoying."

Her frown grew. "I didn't realize... did I say something wrong?"

"No." Skye shook her head. "He was just... he has this stupid conspiracy theory that every girl I talk to is secretly my girlfriend?" She didn't specify that the conspiracy theory only applied to present company. "He was just going to ask if you liked girls which, you know, felt kind of inappropriate for book club introductions."

"Oh." Sadie said. "For the record, I'm not uncomfortable with your friends knowing I like girls. You can tell them."

Skye almost fell out of her chair. "You what?"

"I mean, presumably they're fine with you liking girls so I don't see what—"

"You like girls?"

Sadie tilted her head to the side. "Yes?"

"Sadie!" Skye slammed her hand down against the desk. "What the fuck! How did I not know that?"

Her eyes narrowed. "I thought you did?"

"How? You literally never talk about girls."

"Or guys. I kind of never leave my house, remember? But I like both, I think. I'm not sure? I don't get book crushes or celebrity crushes or anything but I'm pretty sure I just like all kinds of people? Obviously at least the girl part though."

"You constantly write love stories about straight couples! What about that could've possibly made the girl part the most obvious?"

Sadie just shrugged as if she wasn't in the process of rewiring Skye's entire brain. "I mean, they're fake and you're real so that's probably the part that's more likely to be accurate, right?"

"I'm... what?"

She just kept tilting her head and staring through the screen. "Would your friends be weird about that?"

"No! I'm... you like girls?" Skye triple checked.

"Yes."

"You like... me?"

Sadie laughed. "Yes?"

All of her nerve endings simultaneously exploded. "You can't just blurt something like that out casually! Oh my god."

"I mean, I've been sending you love letters for years now. I thought that was kind of... a very established thing."

"It absolutely wasn't!"

"Oh," she said. "Sorry. I figured it was irrelevant to bring up for a bit because you'd said Isaac was gay and then that she was a girl so I thought you guys liked each other until I realized I'd gotten the gay part wrong and then I just..." she shrugged. "I don't know. I thought you knew."

"I didn't—" Skye froze. If finding out Sadie liked her (not just in that moment, but that she had for years) had sent her heart soaring, it had now taken up residence somewhere in her left foot. "Shit," she said. "Shit, I didn't..." she pulled out her phone. "Isaac's not out yet. I'm supposed to be the only... you're not supposed to know."

Sadie's brow furrowed. "The rest of your friends don't?"

She shook her head.

"I don't think I said anything. I umm... kind of didn't say much of anything so it should be fine. I can just pretend I don't—"

"What? No. I'm literally already texting her, she obviously needs to know." Skye chewed at her cheek. "I'm not sure... it's my fault. You didn't do anything wrong, I was just being an idiot, but I think I need to talk to her about book club stuff before we decide if we're going through with the next meeting? I obviously trust you but it's not up to me to do that here so I think I need to see if—"

"Right," Sadie stopped her. "Right, yeah of course. We can talk later if you need to—"

"Yeah, that's probably smartest." She glanced back at her phone. "See you."

She slammed the laptop shut, let herself pace around her room exactly three times, and threw on her jacket. Isaac hadn't responded yet, but she figured she might as well start heading over now. This was the kind of visit that required a bakery pitstop.

From: Sadie
To: Skye

Today I heard that this book I like is getting adapted into a movie
and my first thought was "I should tell Skye" then I realized
you've never read it before and probably wouldn't even want to
watch the movie and there was absolutely no reason news about a
random movie based on a random book you've never read should
have made me think about you, but it did.

I've realized I just subconsciously associate you with everything
that makes me happy. I think that's pretty great.

From: Skye
To: Sadie

Sknhfdksfskfnsklnfdknd you know I now absolutely have to read
whatever book this is so I can be appropriately hyped for whatever
movie you're talking about, right?

I already realized it, but just for the record, I very consciously want
to know everything about all the things that make you happy
because I think you're cool as fuck.

Unlike the rest of their friend group, Isaac and Skye did not meet on the first day of ninth grade. They'd gone to elementary school together. Skye had punched her in the face.

It was nothing personal and thankfully, Isaac realized that. While Skye would grow up to realize that she definitely approached quite a few things too violently as a kid, she still believed that she was never without cause. Except for Isaac.

They'd been sharing story predictions in second grade. Skye had been sent to the hall for interrupting one too many times, and walked back in just in time to hear Isaac blurt out the same guess she'd been trying to make to receive praise instead of punishment. So, she'd punched her. Marched right across the carpet to do it then went straight back to the hall before anyone could kick her out.

It wasn't until she got off of suspension and her parents gave up on lecturing her for it that she realized that Isaac had never done anything wrong. So at recess, she walked back over, held out a hand, and for the first time in her life, Skye Eaton apologized and meant it.

"You can punch me back, if you want," she'd offered.

Isaac had just looked confused. "No thank you."

And that was that. They never interacted again. Punching everyone's favourite student was a very good way to assure you'd never end up in the same class. Then, on the first day of ninth grade, Isaac had decided to give her another chance anyway. Skye wasn't sure how many more times she could ask her to do that.

Isaac's smile dropped the moment she opened her door. "What did you do?"

Skye swayed from foot to foot on her doorstep. "How did you—"

"You brought a whole plate of brownies. I only get brownies when you fuck up."

Skye blushed. "Did you not want—"

"I obviously want the brownies," she snatched the plate out of her arms. "Come on," she sighed. "Come fill me in."

Skye sat on her favourite of Isaac's basement couches, picking at the peeling fake leather as Isaac processed what she'd told her. Isaac did all her thinking inside her head. It had a tendency to make Skye's skin itch.

"You outed me to your internet girlfriend," she finally said.

Skye winced. "I don't think I ever like, intentionally said you were trans. I just... in my mind she'd never talk to anyone we knew so I haven't been pronoun switching and—"

"She lives like two streets away from here."

She swallowed. "I know. I suck, I'm sorry. I wasn't thinking."

"You weren't."

Isaac took a deep breath, running a hand through her hair.

"She promised she won't tell anyone."

"Has she already?"

"No! Or... I don't think so. I'll check."

She just sighed again.

"Hey," Skye leaned forward. "It'll be fine, okay? We've literally only had one meeting. We can cancel it and blame it on low attendance or something and then there's no reason for her to even have the opportunity to mess up. And then in a few months we'll be in Toronto and out and it won't even be possible for me to keep fucking up."

"Are we even still going to Toronto?"

"What?" Skye's forehead scrunched up. "Of course. Why would we?"

"The girl you're obsessed with definitely isn't."

Skye rolled her eyes. "Sadie's great, but it's not like being physically close by makes it any easier to hangout with her. I can still call her from Toronto."

Isaac watched her for a long moment before nodding. "And what if I decide not to be out in Toronto?"

"Then I'll get way better at this. No one else knows, I swear. I just... sometimes I forget Sadie's not some story I made up? Which is stupid, but I swear I haven't accidentally told anyone else. She gets it's a messy situation so if we asked her to say she can't come to meetings anymore, I'm sure she'd be fine with that."

Isaac rolled her eyes. "She's the whole reason we have a club."

"We can start a new one then."

"It's fine. As long as you don't think she might randomly—"

"She won't."

Isaac shrugged. "It's fine then."

Skye watched her carefully. "You're sure?"

"I mean, I'd rather you didn't out me to anyone else but if it's already done, I guess we'll deal with it."

Skye pressed her fists against her forehead. "I'm so sorry."

"I know," Isaac said. "We're fine." Not it's fine, because it wasn't and they both knew it.

"She's gay so I'm sure she wouldn't—she told me I could tell you guys that, by the way. I didn't just fuck up twice. She somehow kept that from me for years so I'm sure—"

"Sadie's gay?" Isaac cut her off.

"Yeah, apparently. Not like, lesbian gay but definitely some kind of queer."

"The girl you've been obsessed with for years likes girls and you've been here for a whole ten minutes without mentioning that?"

"We had more pressing issues to deal with! I obviously wasn't going to—"

Isaac slapped her forehead. "Always lead with good news, Skye. This would have been so much more fun if I'd known I could tease you about it the whole time."

She blushed. "In that case she umm... I think she likes me. No, know. She like, very overtly said she's liked me for like, a while now."

Isaac threw a pillow at her. She caught it with her face. "You have a girlfriend now and you were just going to—"

"She's not my girlfriend! She's my friend who just happens to be a girl and..." she trailed off.

"Your friend who just happens to be a girl who happens to like you who you happen to like back?" Isaac finished for her.

Skye rolled her eyes. "It's not that simple."

"It's very literally the simplest thing that's ever happened to you." She reached across the coffee table to smack Skye's knee. "How the hell did you fumble this?"

She shrugged. "I don't know, it's not like I could've just asked her out."

"Yes, you could've! You can have like... cute little Skype dates."

"Well she didn't ask me out either, so..."

"Does she know you're obsessed with her?"

Skye thought about it for a moment. "Oh."

Isaac gaped. She snatched the pillow off of Skye's lap just to throw it at her again.

"I got distracted! And then I came over here so we hung up pretty quickly and—"

Isaac stood up and pointed towards the stairs. "Get out of my house."

"I—"

"The girl you're obsessed with said she liked you back and you hung up on her? Get out of here and call her back right now."

Skye chewed on her lip. "We don't have another Skype scheduled so she's probably—"

"Call her!"

She sighed, pulling her phone out of her pocket. She met Isaac's eye. "I do this right now and if she says no, we go do something stupid then never bring this conversation up ever again."

"Deal."

The phone rang. The answering machine clicks on, but Isaac kept gesturing at the phone. Skye swallowed a sigh.

"Hey, it's Skye," she said. "I think I hung up before... I also like girls, obviously. And you. Mostly just you." Her finger missed the end call button the first three times she tried to hit it. She really hoped the answering machine didn't catch Isaac laughing her ass off.

Skye: *Hey!*

Skye: *Not sure if you got my message yet but if not maybe listen to it? And get back to me ASAP? The suspense is kind of killing me here.*

Skye stayed by her phone constantly, but no calls came that night. For the first time in years, her email was completely empty.

The skype invite came through on her computer while she was studying the next evening. She clicked it within milliseconds.

"Hi," Sadie took over her screen. "How was your day?"

"Good," Skye said a bit too quickly. "Boring. How was yours?"

"Fine." She shrugged. "I got your message."

Skye blushed.

"Was that one of those 'friends dare you to ask someone out' messages or—"

"What? No. I mean, kind of? I was with Isaac, but I do like you. I didn't even ask you out."

"Oh," she said. "That's good."

"I mean, obviously I meant to."

Sadie frowned. "I can't go out."

"Right, yeah, of course, but we could video chat or something. If you wanted to."

"We already are."

"Right, but..." Skye sighed. "I like you and you like me so maybe we keep video chatting except this time we're also dating?"

She kept frowning, tilting her head. "There's a very good chance I'll never see you in person."

"That's fine. People have internet partners all the time. We can just be internet partners who also live close enough to each other to not waste money on shipping gifts and shit."

"Internet couples meet up. We'd just... keep doing this. Nothing would really change so there's not really a point. It's not fair to you to—"

"Sadie, I'm asking you out because I really, really, like you and I want to officially like you. I'm not secretly hoping you'll say no."

She thought about it for a moment before smiling. "Yes? Okay?"

"Yeah?"

"Sure. We're now officially Skyping non-platonically."

They both grinned.

Sadie: Goodnight <3

Sadie: Sorry, was that weird to send?

Skye: <3<3<3<3<3<3<3<3<3<3<3<3<3<3<3<3<3<3<3<3<3<3<3<3<3 <3<3<3<3<3<3<3<3<3<3<3<3<3<3<3<3<3<3<3<3<3<3<3<3<3<3<3

Skye: <3<3<3<3<3<3<3<3<3<3<3<3<3<3<3<3<3<3<3<3<3<3<3<3<3<3 <3<3<3<3<3<3<3<3<3

Skyping non-platonically ended up consisting mostly of sitting in the same video call while they worked in silence on other things, but that worked perfectly for Skye. If they couldn't inhabit the same place, they'd inhabit the same screen. Sometimes, she'd get home from school, turn her computer on before she'd even finished pulling out her homework, and then keep it on until she fell asleep.

And it felt good. It felt really, really, good.

Sadie: Skye, it's fine. I get it.

Skye: <3<3<3<3<3<3<3<3<3<3<3<3<3<3<3<3<3<3<3<3<3<3<3<3<3<3<3 <3<3<3<3<3<3<3<3<3<3<3<3<3<3<3<3<3<3<3<3<3<3<3<3<3<3<3 <3<3<3<3<3<3<3<3<3<3<3<3<3<3<3<3<3<3<3<3<3<3<3<3<3<3<3 <3<3<3<3<3<3<3<3<3<3<3<3<3<3<3<3<3<3<3<3<3<3<3<3<3<3<3 <3<3<3<3<3<3<3<3<3<3<3<3<3<3<3<3<3<3<3<3<3<3<3<3<3<3<3 <3<3<3<3<3<3<3<3<3<3<3<3<3<3<3<3<3<3<3<3<3<3<3

Skye: >:)

"Are you biasing your book club for me?" Sadie asked.

Skye had been highlighting her chem textbook, so it took a moment for the question to click. "What?"

They'd finished their third book club meeting earlier that day and had officially announced the booklist of entirely Sadie's picks, but Skye was too focused to realize that that's what she was asking about.

"There's no way everything random chosen just happened to be the things I suggested. If you're biasing it because we're dating that's also probably not good but if it's because everyone thinks there's something wrong with me, you need to tell them—"

"The club's a sham, remember?" Skye technically didn't lie. "You're the only one who actually has book opinions, so we decided to just go with yours."

"Oh," she said. "Okay, good."

Skye hesitated. "There's... there has to be something though, right? I know you obviously don't want to talk about it but there must be..." she sighed. "People don't just not leave the house for seventeen years. If... you don't have to tell me, but I guess I just need you to know that I'd really like to know? I promise I won't be weird about it if it's an anxiety thing or an illness thing or something, I just care about you and would rather not be caught of guard if it's something that could abruptly go really—"

"It's not. I'm fine."

"Okay," Skye pretended to believe her. She wanted to push, but she was too scared she'd end the call. And maybe even more scared of what the answer would be.

"And I haven't... I do go outside. Sometimes. I'm just not a crowd person."

"Okay," Skye nodded. She didn't listen to the voice screaming at her to remind Sadie that she didn't count as a crowd. For once, Skye Eaton stayed silent. "That's fine."

They both got back to work.

From: Sadie
To: Skye

Meet me at the entrance to the trail down the street from my house at 10pm tomorrow.

Skye tried to call her. She didn't pick up.

"We don't have to meet anywhere." She told the answering machine. "It's seriously fine, okay?"

She texted back within a minute.

Sadie: *I want to. Meet me.*
Skye: *???*
Skye: *ur sure?*
Skye: *is this safe?*
Sadie: *Yes.*
Skye: *Promise?*
Sadie: *Yes.*
Skye: *see u tomorrow then.*

Skye didn't pay attention to a fucking thing all day.

She got half a note down first period before switching to random undecipherable pencil sketches drawn between checking her phone under the table to make sure none of her "are you sure?" texts were answered with a "no." She sat silent in the cafeteria, knee bouncing a mile a minute, doing such a bad job pretending to pay attention to her surroundings that every single one of her friends pulled her aside at least once to ask if something was wrong. She shouldn't have come to school at all. She might as well have stayed home where she could at least freak out within the safety of her own bedroom or maybe even try to sleep through the day to rush to the night.

She was well aware that something could have been wrong. She wasn't stupid enough to not be suspicious of the girl who'd adamantly insisted they never met up face to face suddenly suggesting they do it long after sundown in what was basically a forest, she was just too excited to give in to that suspicion.

So, after school, she biked straight home, pretended to be present enough to study and took out her textbooks, then sat at her desk for hours, waiting for night to come.

Her parents were smart enough to know that the world should fear her, not the other way around, so when she slipped out the door at nine thirty claiming she was going to Isaac's, they didn't bat an eye.

She didn't take her bike. It would have been faster, but she was terrified that something would go wrong and she'd be stuck trying to carry both it and Sadie to the nearest emergency services. Or that everything would go right and Sadie wouldn't have a bike and would use Skye's as an excuse to split up early. If she had one night to be with Sadie, she was going to milk it for every possible second.

Even walking, even though she went first to the elementary school then around to the front of Sadie's house to make sure she chose the right trail entrance, she was way too early. Waiting alone in a dark trail felt dangerous but so did pacing around in front of it and though Skye liked to think that she wasn't insecure about anything about herself, she suddenly really, really, didn't want Sadie seeing her before she got to see Sadie. She stepped past the entrance, tried and failed to make herself sit down on a giant rock, and went back to pacing.

Then, at ten (exactly at ten) she saw her.

Sadie O'Brian was wearing big yellow rainboots despite the dry earth beneath her feet. She was had on blue jeans beneath a long, flowing, pink dress covered by a trench coat that was slightly too big for her. Her hair was still in a braid. She was walking towards her at a fairly normal pace with a fairly normal gait and despite the dress-jeans-rainboots combo and the fact that she was Sadie O'Brian, she seemed unbelievably ordinary.

Skye made herself stop pacing. It didn't seem like Sadie'd noticed her yet, so she waited for her to also enter the path before saying, "hi."

Sadie spun around. Her eyes met Skye's and for the first time, there was nothing but air between them. She smiled and opened her mouth to say something back, but never got there.

Skye had enough time to watch a single stone fall out from a pocket in her skirt before Sadie went drifting up into the air.

Nonymous

Nonymous

Sadie O'Brian's (incredibly brief) Superhero Origin Story

Nonymous

When Sadie O'Brian was born, she came out crying, screaming, and floating towards the ceiling. If not for the umbilical cord, she probably would have crashed into it.

Her parents pulled her down, smuggled her out of the hospital, and then never let her leave the house again.

From the moment Sadie O'Brian was born, she was fucking incredible.

Nonymous

122

Nonymous

Sadie

Nonymous

There was once a girl with a hand wrapped around her ankle.

It wasn't supposed to be there but then, the girl wasn't supposed to be either. She shouldn't have come. She was supposed to stay locked away in her tower, waiting for rescue. But sometimes, rescuers took too long to get the hint.

The hand on her ankle felt like it was pulling down, but the girl knew that that wasn't true. She, against all science and logic, was pulling up. And she—despite what she lacked in size and strength and desire—was winning. She'd tied string through the loops in her boots. She'd practiced dozens of times at home to assure that they would hold tight. But the floating girl hadn't calculated for the hand on her ankle so as she pulled up, the hand pushed against the string until it came loose and sent a tiny cascade of pebbles falling to the earth.

The girl squeezed her eyes shut. She told herself that she was in an elevator. She told herself that she was picturing it go up floor by floor. It was just the newest trick in hundreds of new tricks from hundreds of new therapists. The girl was good at imagining so in theory, it should have worked. What she wasn't good at was convincing herself that imagining things made them real. For a person currently slowly inching towards the treeline, she was far too practical for her own good. She conjured her elevator, she imagined the floors, but her heart kept hammering and she kept climbing up and up and further still. Finally, she opened her eyes, sighed, and gave up.

"Let go of me," she said. She heard how blunt it sounded. Affect was something she'd practiced and mastered years ago, but it was hard to focus on much else when one was trying to keep oneself grounded. Still, she regretted the bluntness.

"What? No." Came the voice from beneath her. The floating girl did not let herself look towards it. She knew it would only push them higher. This had never been a good idea. "You're... holy shit is this real? Are you fucking flying?"

"Let go," she repeated. Her stomach twisted. Her heart felt nauseous. This was what floating girls got when they tried to rewrite their stories. A lost boot and a hand on their ankles and far more seen than they'd ever wanted to be. They were climbing higher still. The floating girl knew that she'd never gone high enough to hurt herself before, but she'd never been carrying non-floating passengers.

"I don't think I should... are you going to fucking fly away or something? Because then I should probably hold on, right? Holy—"

"You need to let go!" She screamed. That was new.

The owner of the hand at her ankle was silent and the floating girl thought that she was finally about to see reason and give in, but then she realized: they were descending. She raised two fingers to her neck, just to confirm that her heart was still hammering. This was new too.

She stayed rigid and still until they reached the ground, terrified that any slight movement would undo whatever had brought them down and send her shooting back up towards the sky. The moment her toes touched the earth and she realized that there was no longer a hand on her ankle, she took off running.

She heard someone calling for her as she went. It was all the more reason to get away.

There was once a girl hidden in a forest.

Really, it was a thin patch of trees wedged between two streets, but forest felt more fitting, especially in the dark. She'd strayed from the path, but to her, it didn't count as straying. She knew every inch of these forests. They were some of the only parts of the outside world she felt safe in.

But now, she was hidden. Crouched down beside a stream with twigs caught in her braid and toes going numb through her bootless sock. She would have poured the stones out of her other boot to help her move more quickly, but even now, she could feel herself being pulled skyward. She squeezed her eyes shut and tried to measure her breathing. She imagined elevators then bubbles then birthday cakes but none of them felt real, so she started tapping a fist against her chest. Sometimes, the floating girl could restart her heart manually.

Her phone chimed. Again and again and again and she knew who must have been messaging her, so she left it dutifully in her pocket and tried to ignore the noise. It didn't work. When the floating girl was approaching weightlessness, sounds got louder. She felt each chime in her ribs.

Ignoring the phone had been the wrong choice. She'd detested the sound because it was grating, but she hadn't realized its true evils. It was a beacon.

"Sadie."

She heard the girl. The one with the dark hair and wide eyes who dealt in cookies and curse words. She heard her sneakers against the crunching leaves and her ragged breath and her own name on her voice. She could not let herself see her.

The floating girl stood up; eyes locked on the tiny creek. "Don't."

Leaves crunched behind her. She couldn't tell if the sound had gotten closer or further.

"Are you okay? Does stuff like that umm... was that..."

Her heels rose off the ground. She counted backwards from ten and managed to push them back down.

"I can't look at you right now." The floating girl said.

"Okay."

"Are you looking at me?"

"Yes?" The girl said. Then, "I could not be?"

"Do that."

There was more crunching.

"You're not looking?" The floating girl checked.

"Sitting against a tree facing a completely different direction. My ass is freezing and everything."

The floating girl took four measured breaths before sitting back down.

"This was a bad idea," she said. "I'm sorry. I should have realized it wasn't a good idea to meet."

"This..." the other girl paused. "Just so we're clear, we're talking about flying right now? You can fucking fly?"

"I float," she corrected.

"You're not fucking with me? You can actually fly?"

"Float," she reiterated. "I wish it was a joke, but—"

"Why would you do that? That's like, every single kid's number one dream!"

The floating girl's nails scraped against dirt and roots. She took three breaths. "I can't even leave the house."

"Oh, shit," the other girl said. "Are you going to fly away or something? Is this dangerous? We could—"

"I've never gone higher than the trees. I think it caps out somewhere around there."

"Then it's still awesome. You should go out more. Hell, they'd probably give you your own TV show if—"

"I don't want people to know!" She winced at the sound of her own raised voice. Curled her fingers further to try and keep her hold on the ground. She stayed seated. She was quiet because she was trying to regain control of her breathing. She didn't know why the other girl also waited before speaking.

"I won't tell anyone," the other girl said. "If that's why you freaked out."

"You can't."

"Okay, I won't," she said. "Seriously. It's not like anyone would believe me."

She heard leaves crunch again, this time definitely getting louder. She flinched. "I said don't come closer."

"No, you said don't look."

"But you're looking to come closer."

The other girl sighed. The crunching stopped. "You're right. I'm sorry. Sitting back down now," she narrated. "A whole few feet away."

The floating girl was quiet. She was used to being quiet here.

"What now?" The other girl asked. "What comes next?"

"You can leave first," the floating girl decided. She would have to because if the floating girl tried to leave knowing that she was still there, she wouldn't be able to keep herself from turning back. "And then I'll go."

"And then we pretend this never happened?"

The floating girl frowned. "Then we both move on with our lives."

She didn't respond so the floating girl added "this was a bad idea." And "I'm sorry."

"What if I don't like that plan?" The other girl finally said.

"I'm sorry," she repeated.

"Nope, that's bullshit. You can fucking fly, Sadie! You don't get to tell me you can do that then expect it to somehow be easier to forget about you."

She winced. "My parents took me to dozens of doctors. I'm not an alien or fairy or mutant or anything. I'm just... an anomaly."

"Okay."

"I don't even control it. It just happens when I get emotional. I get stuck up there for a bit, then come back down when I'm calm."

"You're calm right now?"

She glanced at where her fist was still trying to jumpstart her own heart. "I don't know," she admitted. "I must be."

"You didn't seem calm. When we came down."

She shrugged, though she'd been wonder about the same thing. "Must have been another anomaly."

"Or maybe you did something to get yourself down," the girl suggested. "We can keep meeting up. Test things."

"What?"

She'd been too distracted listening to her talk to track her movements until all at once, there was a hand on her arm.

The floating girl shrieked. In her haste to get away, she jumped to her feet so quickly that she accidentally gave the sky the help it needed.

"Yell at me," the girl said. The girl still holding onto her arm. "Or... try to remember exactly what you said or did or something."

But the floating girl could do none of that. She shook her head rapidly as she slowly started to rise to try and articulate what her tongue could not. Her words and breath and heart all met in her chest and threatened to suffocate her.

"I'm sorry." The hand was off her arm before her head had passed the ten-foot point. She heard her thud as the other girl met the dirt, but didn't let herself look down "I'm sorry."

The apology would soon be too far away for either acceptance or refusal, so the floating girl turned towards the sky and waited to be delivered to it. She squeezed her eyes shut, climbed back into her elevator, and waited to come down.

It took longer than normal to silence her mind. It was spinning, then. Skye Eaton had been making it spin for years, but that normally only happened within the safely of her home where she could rest comfortably against the ceiling. Here, the air was open and she was too high to see anything she could use to distract herself. Here, the girl she was thinking of was down below. Or maybe home, by then. She must have been up in the air for at least half an hour, wind prickling against her face. Surely, Skye was already back at her house. Knowing that was the only way she was able to bring herself back down.

She would hit the ground and run the whole way home before she could lose her footing again. She'd sneak in through the backdoor and bury herself under every blanket she could find even though she already knew that she'd inevitably end up sleeping in the air that night. But then she touched the ground and heard a voice.

"I'm sorry."

The floating girl froze.

"I can go," Skye Eaton said. "If you need me to. I just thought I should... I'm sorry. That was fucked of me."

When her feet stayed flat on the ground, she took a deep breath. "I think I'm fine," she said. "It happens less, when I'm tired. That's why I wanted to meet late."

"Okay. That's good," Skye said. "Not good that you're tired, obviously but... I'm glad you're fine."

She took a step. The floating girl flinched.

"I'm not going to grab you again," she said. "Promise."

She didn't know how to explain that that was all she wanted. How desperate she was to be connected to something grounded. With Skye though, that would clearly never work.

"Okay," the floating girl said. "That's good to know."

"I shouldn't have done it. I mean, the first time, absolutely. I feel like you get a pass when the girl you like floats away the first time you get to see her. But the second..." she sighed. "I'm sorry. I'm an idiot, sometimes. I's not happening again."

"Okay."

"I can go," Skye said. "If you need me to."

She wished she'd said want. That way, she wouldn't be lying when she said "No, that's okay. I think..." she felt for her pulse again. Still close enough to normal. "I'm pretty sure I'll be fine now. If nothing exciting happens."

"I'll try my best to be boring then."

She squeezed her eyes shut as she turned around just in case, but her heart remained in her chest. When she opened them, Skye was closer than she'd thought she'd been. Her dark brown hair was tangled from the wind.

"Here," she extended an arm towards her. "You lost a shoe."

There was once a girl being watched in a forest.

She stared forward and the girl walking beside her was trying her best to be subtle about it, but she could feel the heat of worried eyes darting towards her every few seconds.

"Can you stop it?" She finally broke. "I said I was fine."

"I wasn't doing anything."

"You're... looking."

"Yeah, because I never get to do that in person."

"Oh."

They walked to the edge of the forest then back again. The girl's toes ached against the stones in her right boot, but that didn't make it feel any less magical. Some of her favourite fairy tales followed heroines whose every step pained them.

"I can stop," Skye said.

She considered it. "No thank you." She wasn't going to look straight at her again though. Counteracting a curse required baby steps.

"Have you always flown?"

"Floated," the girl corrected. "And yes."

"Do you know why?"

"No."

"And that's why you don't leave your house?"

"I leave," she corrected again. "Just when there aren't a lot of people around."

She felt something hit her shoulder. It went both sore and hot. It felt good against the night air.

"I thought you were fucking dying!" Skye exclaimed. "You could have told me—"

"That I have superpowers?"

"Okay, fair. But you could have liked... shown me."

"I wasn't planning on it. This was a mistake."

"I won't tell anyone," Skye reiterated.

"I know," the girl said. She did. She'd known there was a chance of floating tonight. She wouldn't have come if she didn't trust Skye completely.

"Then why are you freaking out?"

"I'm not."

Skye sighed. "You're speed-limping away from me with one boot in your hand and the other full of rocks. That seems like—"

The floating girl spun around. When she looked right at Skye, she couldn't tell if it was her heart or head that felt like it was about to disobey gravity, so she shifted her gaze just past her left shoulder. "I like you," she told the tree behind her.

"Good," Skye said. "I like you too."

"No," the floating girl shook her head. "I mean, I'm obviously never going to be able to like you the proper way. You deserve—"

"I'm ace," Skye interrupted her.

The floating girl cocked her head to the side. "What does that mean?"

"A lot of things," she shrugged. "It depends on the person. But for me, it means I'm never going to be like, into anyone. Sexually. Like romantically, yeah, obviously, but not... that way. And I don't know if I'd want to do stuff like that yet, so if we're going by some arbitrary definition of liking people properly or typically or the way the mass majority of people are expected to or whatever, I can't do that either."

The floating girl took a deep breath. "I can't even look at you right now," she whispered.

"Yeah, but we're talking. That's a step in the right direction, right?"

"It could just be because I'm tired."

She shrugged again. "Then next time we'll meet up indoors where I don't have to worry about you flying away. You obviously talk to your parents and stuff, right?"

She stuffed her hands into her pockets. Her knuckled brushed against stone. "You're a lot more overwhelming though."

Even with her eyes on the tree, she could see Skye blush.

"My parents don't even know I'm here. They would have known this was an awful idea. You can't just come over."

"You can come to mine."

The floating girl sighed. "That's not even... I came because I thought it would convince you I was normal. I wanted you to think that I was normal."

Skye frowned. "I've never thought you were normal."

She winced at the reminder. "Right. You thought I was from space or something."

"No, shoot. I didn't—that was when I was a little kid. I obviously didn't mean..." she sighed. "You're more than normal, okay? You're unapologetically yourself and crazy open about the things you're interested in and so honest that it's slightly terrifying sometimes. That's better than normal."

She played with the rocks in her pocket. "And now you know I can float."

"True." Skye nodded. "But I didn't know that until like an hour ago and I still liked you then too. Promise I'm not exploiting you for your very cool superpowers."

"They're not—"

"You were as tall as the trees a few minutes ago. Don't you dare try to pretend that wasn't cool as fuck."

A rock pinched her finger.

Skye sighed. "We don't have to meet up in person," she relented. "But you don't get to tell me you're even cooler than I thought you were then disappear."

She considered. "Coming tonight was irresponsible."

Skye nodded. "All the best things are."

"I came down quickly though. That first time. That doesn't normally..." she took a deep breath. Removed her hands from her pockets. "I would like to come to your house this weekend," she declared. "To experiment."

Skye grinned. "That can definitely be arranged."

Nonymous

Nonymous

Skye & Sadie, Sadie & Skye

Nonymous

Skye

Skye hadn't had anyone her parents knew was a girl over since they stopped forcing her to invite them to all her birthday parties at the beginning of middle school, so she tried her best to keep pronouns ambiguous when she told them about her plans with Sadie.

"A new friend's coming over tomorrow," she said during dinner Friday night. The Eaton's were a 'sit down together at mealtime' kind of family so she hoped talking about upcoming plans would seem normal there, but her parents still exchanged a look.

She'd forgotten that it had almost been just as long since she'd had a new friend over too.

"A girl?" Her father asked, eyes twinkling.

She rolled her eyes. "Not that kind of girl." Except yes, exactly that kind of girl. Except they definitely weren't going to be doing whatever her parents might worry about them doing because Sadie couldn't even touch Skye without ending up on the ceiling and if Skye ever did decide she wanted to have sex with someone, it would take a lot longer than two in person meetings.

"Sure," her dad chuckled.

Her mother put a hand on his arm. "Just make sure you guys leave the door open."

"Mom!"

There were moments where she considered telling them that she was ace. They'd been so freakishly cool with her being a lesbian that she sometimes felt guilty for it whenever she talked to other queer people and while she was pretty sure neither of them had any idea what ace meant, she couldn't imagine them being bigots to anyone. But there'd also been the concern. The sit-down meeting after they'd found out where they'd assured her that they "loved her no matter what and even more for trusting them with something like this", but that maybe she should wait a bit to tell other people. Maybe she should make sure that she was absolutely certain she liked girls first. Skye's parents had never been ashamed of her, but they were aware of the way the rest of the world worked. They weren't naïve enough to think that coming out in a small town would ever go smoothly.

Asexuality complicated things. Her parents were fine with her being gay because they truly believed that she was born that way and that it was an unchangeable, undeniable truth about her. It was easy to explain the innate state of existence that was liking girls to someone who'd liked a girl enough to marry her and a girl who'd been liked enough to be married. It was harder to explain an absence of feeling. Difficult to articulate exactly what sexual attraction was when most of the world saw it as a given and impossible to describe how she knew that it wasn't for her.

Until she'd told Sadie the night before, no one had known. Maybe she'd only told her because she knew Sadie had a bigger secret to keep. She trusted her parents with almost everything and Isaac with absolutely everything, but she hadn't even told her because while "ace" and "lesbian" were both labels that she knew the people she cared about would probably be fine with, "ace lesbian" sometimes felt like an anomaly. Lesbianism wasn't a choice, but if other people assumed romantic and sexual attraction went hand in hand, wouldn't it become one? If she didn't experience sexual attraction, how could she be sure that she only liked girls? Why wouldn't she choose the easier option?

Skye was a lesbian and ace and both, but she knew that to most people who weren't, that was seemingly contradictory. So, she stuck with lesbian because it just happened to be the thing that she'd figured out first.

"She's really socially anxious," she decided to argue instead.

Her mother drummed her nails against the table. "Socially anxious girls can still have—"

"Mom!" She exclaimed again.

Her father was trying so hard to supress a laugh that his whole face went red.

"I'm seventeen. Next year I'll be—"

"That's still not eighteen."

Skye played the card. "It's Sadie O'Brian."

All colour left her father's face. Her mother dropped her fork.

"Honey," she said slowly. "Sadie can't—"

"Well, she can and she does but she's not exactly a people person and she won't come over if she knows you guys are going to be creepily spying on us the whole time."

Her parents looked at each other again.

"Are her parents okay with her coming over?" Her mother checked.

Skye rolled her eyes. "She's seventeen too."

"We'd like to talk with them first. Just in case they have any emergency plans we need to—"

"Fine. Whatever. I'll talk to her." Skye pushed back against her chair and picked up her plate. She knew she wasn't being fair. A few days ago, she would have also been concerned about the prospect of Sadie coming over. Sometimes (maybe most of the time, actually) Skye's anger was irrational.

She went to finish eating in her room.

> **Skye:** *my parents want to talk to ur parents b4 you come over*
> **Skye:** *sorry*
> **Skye:** *we can figure something else out if theyre gonna b pissed*
> **Sadie:** *That's fine. They're used to lying for me.*
> **Skye:** *arent they gonna know I know?*
> **Sadie:** *They already do. I told them the morning after we met.*
> **Skye:** *were they pissed?*
> **Sadie:** *Worried, I think.*
> **Sadie:** *What's your parents' number?*

Skye couldn't quite tell if it was an intentional subject change, but she sent it along anyway and didn't ask any more follow up questions just in case.

She put her phone down, lied back on her bed, then instantly jumped back up again. Her friends were slobs and her parents had given up on trying to force her to clean her room years ago, but if Sadie was coming over, she needed to at least pretend to be a functional human being. She had a lot of work to do.

Sadie

There was once a girl with two feet on the sidewalk.

If her heels lifted every few steps, it was only because there was a spring in them. She counted each segment of sidewalk as she went to make sure she remained firmly attached to it.

This was a bad idea, but she didn't let herself think it. She suspected that the best way to fight her curse was to keep her head entirely empty, but she'd never been that good at that. Skye's house was unreachable through the trails and backroads that she was more comfortable on, but she told herself that that didn't matter. She'd test ran things like this before. Walked through populated parks with her parents holding onto her from either side, just in case she started to float away. They'd offered to walk her to Skye's, but she'd refused. If she was going to become a great writer, she had to see the rest of the world first. She couldn't do that if she always let them anchor her.

She didn't drift more than an inch off the ground the entire walk over but when she was suddenly right there, waiting for Skye's door to open, she felt herself go weightless. She desperately grabbed the knocker and pressed up against it, hoping Skye would answer instead of her parents.

She did.

"Hey," Skye frowned when opening the door pulled the floating girl in with it. "My parents are out."

The floating girl nodded, took a shaking breath, and stepped past the threshold to let Skye close the door behind her. In a few seconds, her feet were a foot off the ground.

"Holy shit," she heard Skye whisper. "Can you umm... move? Is it like swimming or something?"

"It's easier when I'm high enough to press against the ceiling," the floating girl tried to explain. "I should be down soon though. This is a small one."

"Try yelling," Skye suggested.

"What?"

"That worked last time, right? Try yelling."

"I don't want to yell at you."

"Cool. Now do that louder and angrier."

The floating girl knew it wouldn't be that easy, but she really wanted to believe that it could be. "I don't want to yell at you!"

They both waited. Nothing happened.

"It was worth a shot," Skye shrugged. "Should I um... pull you somewhere? Is that rude? I don't know floating person etiquette."

The floating girl sucked on her lip. "It normally would be fine but I don't think... touching you definitely isn't going to help me calm down."

Skye blushed. She did that a lot. Sadie liked it each and every time. She hoped Skye didn't notice when she moved half an inch higher.

"Guess we'll just have to wait then," Skye said.

"Your parents—"

"Won't be home for hours. We're fine."

"What if they get back early?"

"They won't."

She didn't know how she was supposed to trust that. She never should have let herself come to this strange house where complete strangers could walk in and learn her secret at any second.

"Stop worrying. They're all the way across town. They promised to text me if they were coming home early."

"I'm not—"

"You got even higher, Sadie."

The floating girl looked down. Sure even, she was quickly approaching the two-foot mark. She squeezed her eyes shut.

"Ask me a math question."

"What?"

"Just do it."

"What's two plus two?"

The floating girl's eyes snapped open. "A hard one."

Skye didn't change the question until her eyes were closed again.

"What's fifty-one times fifty-one?"

She started to solve it, then stopped. "Don't help me."

"Okay."

"Or talk until I get it."

"Sure."

She parted her lips slightly to breath through them while she tried to solve it. When she finally opened her eyes a few minutes later, she was back on the ground. Skye was watching her, so she said, "one thousand six hundred and one."

Skye grinned. "I got it like two minutes ago, for the record."

The floating girl's smile was uneasy, but it was still a smile.

"Come on," Skye took off. "My room's this way."

The floating girl had always thought that rooms were extensions of the people they belonged to, but maybe that was because it made a pretty literary device. If she'd written Skye Eaton's room, it would have been every colour all at once. It would be overflowing in so many random knickknacks that it would have been impossible to ever properly catalogue it. The real Skye Eaton's room was just that: a room. A blue-sheeted bed in the middle and mint green walls. A desk beside a messy bookshelf full of textbooks, children's novels, and the odd paper or notebook and a pile of miscellaneous clothes and blankets in the corner. Skye watched her survey it.

"We should have gone to yours," she said. "If your parents already know I know that was probably the safer idea, right?"

The floating girl winced. She didn't know why she hadn't realized that herself. She was getting reckless. Or maybe she'd really wanted to learn whatever story she'd been certain that Skye Eaton's bedroom would tell her.

"We'll do that next time," she said.

Skye smiled.

"What?" She knew better than to discount smiles from pretty girls.

"Next time," Skye said. "I like it when you're not trying to get rid of me."

She winced. "I'm not... it wasn't that."

Skye nodded. "I know." She sat down cross-legged on her bed. The floating girl looked around the room, but the only other seat available was the desk chair and since she hadn't been given permission to sit there, she stayed standing.

"So," Skye clapped her hand. "The flying."

"Floating."

"Yeah, whatever. The floating. That's been happening your whole life?"

She nodded. "Since I was born."

"And your parents weren't part of like, some kind of top secret government research project?"

The floating girl frowned. She licked her lips. "I'm not a science experiment. My parents didn't want me to be like this."

"Right, obviously, but maybe they were part of something else and this is like, a side effect or something?"

She squeezed her eyes open and shut before responding. It was important for floating girls to always stay calm, especially around dark-haired girls who made them want to be everything but. "I'm not a science experiment." She repeated.

There must have been some miscalculation. Some tonal indicator she'd missed that let a bit too much of herself leak through to the surface. Skye put her arms up in surrender and she checked to make sure she wasn't floating again, but she was still on the ground.

"Okay, fair. Dropping it." Skye tugged on her sweater sleeves. "For the record, I'm trying my best to handle all of this properly, but I'm going to keep fucking up. I found out people could fly a few days ago, Sadie. That's going to take a bit to handle properly."

The floating girl took a step backwards. This had always been a bad idea. "I'm sorry. I can—"

"Don't go. That wasn't me telling you to go."

She swallowed, staring at the carpet. "I'm a lot," she said. "To come to terms with. I'm... it's a lot. You don't have to—"

"I've been a lot my entire life, Sadie. You're fine. Stay. I was just saying I'm probably going to keep fucking up, so stay and tell me next time I do."

The floating girl swallowed. The floating girl stayed.

"So," Skye continued. "You float, you always have, you don't know why, and it happens when you get upset."

"When I get emotional," she corrected. "It doesn't have to be upset."

"What does it feel like?"

"What?"

"The floating. Does it just like... happen?"

Sadie closed her eyes. She knew exactly what it felt like, but sometimes she had trouble making the words she said match up with the thoughts in her head. Things were easier to deal with when she could turn one of her other senses off. "It's not really like a pull," she decided. "I think it's a push? My toes go fuzzy then my knees then it works its way up to my head and has no where else to go and it pushes against the top of my skull and then I'm floating."

"Is it uncomfortable?"

"It's..." she considered. "I don't know. Fuzzy." When she opened her eyes again, there was a notebook in Skye's hands.

"You're taking notes."

Skye looked up at her and frowned. "You're floating again, Sade."

She knew that she was. She didn't need her telling her that she was. "You're taking notes on me," she repeated.

Skye put her pencil down and closed the book. "I won't show anyone," she said slowly.

"That's not even—you're studying me!" She didn't have to find her pulse to know that it was picking up again. She'd be ceiling bound no matter what.

"Yeah," Skye said. "You asked me to."

"I didn't ask you to study me." She kept her fists tight and her voice tighter. She couldn't let herself get stuck here. She wouldn't let herself lose control in Skye Eaton's bedroom. "Why would you think it was okay to—"

She didn't lose control first though. Skye did. "You fucking asked to come over to experiment with your powers!"

"That doesn't mean you get to treat me like one!"

The air went tense. They stared at each other.

"Sadie..." Skye said.

"I know," she squeezed her eyes shut. "I know."

Her feet were both back on the ground.

Skye

"It's yelling then."

"It's not. That didn't work earlier."

It sure fucking seemed like it was yelling.

"Maybe it's getting mad," Skye suggested.

Sadie just shook her head. "That doesn't make sense. I start floating when I get mad. It can't cause it and stop it at the same time."

She knew it wasn't the most pressing issue, but maybe she asked it because she was a little mad herself. Skye'd already had enough people in her life get mad at her for no reason. That wasn't supposed to also come from Sadie.

"You are though, right? Mad?"

Sadie sighed. She crossed her arms over her chest. "This was a bad idea. I should—"

Skye jumped up. She didn't get to get freak out at her for no reason and then just go. "No! You don't get to get pissed at me for trying to help then storm out."

"I'm not storming," Sadie said. "I don't do that, as a general rule. It makes me—"

"Then you don't get to eerily calmly leave either!"

She sighed again. "I'm not—I don't..." she frowned and pulled out her phone.

Skye's whole body flashed hot. "You can't just fucking ignore me in the middle of—"

Sadie held up a finger. Skye was crushing just hard enough to actually wait.

After a bit more typing, Sadie held out her phone.

Can we text?

Skye's eyes narrowed. "You're literally right here. We can't just—"

Sadie's shoulders tensed. Skye watched her heels begin to rise.

"Okay," she quickly corrected, pulling out her own phone. "Okay. We'll text."

You don't have to, the next text read. *I'm just bad at talking sometimes.*

Ok

You don't have to text too.

that's fine

You're kind of a slow typer though.

Skye laughed. Sadie briefly looked up at her.

Sorry.

"No, that's fair."

Are you mad at me?

"Are you going to keep getting pissed over things you didn't tell me weren't cool?"

I might.

Skye rolled her eyes.

I can try not to.

"Then we're fine. You have to tell me when I'm fucking up though. I'd rather you not spend forever on my ceiling."

It took a while for the next message to come through.

I want to figure this out. Just maybe less clinically. We probably don't need notes and stuff, right?

"They're your superpowers." Skye shrugged.

Stop calling it that too.

"Got it."

There was another long pause. *I don't want to only see you when we're figuring this out. I know I'm the one who said that was what we should do today so it's fine if that's all you wanted to do, but I don't think I can keep meeting up in person if we're only ever going to talk about the floating.*

Skye rolled her eyes. "I literally just used it as an excuse to get you to keep putting up with me. We can watch TV or something? No floating or talking required?"

Sadie looked around the room. *It still might happen. Your parents could get home and see.*

"We can just watch on my laptop." She waited for her to nod before getting up to grab it from her desk. She set it up at the foot of her bed. When she turned around, Sadie was still hovering.

Skye rolled her eyes. "You can sit, you know. Promise to refrain from touching or talking or anything else hot enough to be float-worthy."

She obviously didn't want Sadie to go shooting back towards the ceiling, but she'd be lying if she said she didn't feel at least a little bit flattered when her heels rose at that.

Sadie

There was once a girl whose very existence meant that her parents were always on edge.

"How was it?" Her father jumped off the couch the moment the door closed behind the floating girl.

"Everything went okay?" Her mother added.

The floating girl made herself smile. It was the least she could do. "I had fun." It wasn't a lie, though just wondering if the same was true for Skye was dangerous. The floating girl had gone too loud then too quiet then had sat on her bed for hours without so much as looking at her. She hadn't even been able to say goodbye out loud when she'd left. But the floating girl had had fun. She focused on that.

"Did you..." her mother trailed off. It had been years, but both of her parents were still uncomfortable saying it. As if the word itself would send her up and away.

"A few times," she nodded. "Yes."

Both adults' eyes widened. It was how she knew that floating couldn't have been genetic. When they wore their emotions, there were never any consequences.

"It was fine," she tried to reassure them. "She already knew about it."

"Just because it seemed fine once doesn't mean—"

"It was fine."

Both of her parents fell silent and smiling at that. She knew that they were well intentioned. She knew that they were just worried that being anything other than pleasant would make the floating girl also become anything other than pleasant and that they all knew what that led to. Their home was safe though. She was just as used to the ceilings there as the floors. She sometimes wished that they'd let themselves get argue with her. At least then she'd have something to argue against.

"I want to have her over soon."

Her parents looked at each other.

"Sweetheart..." her father started. "I'm not sure if—"

"It's riskier there," she explained. Facts were sometimes more threatening to her father than feelings. "Her parents were out but they might not be next time. It makes more sense for her to come here."

Her father frowned. "Maybe we should just stop—"

"I can't just never be around people. I'm old enough to live on my own next year."

They looked at each other again. Her parents spoke a whole different language that they'd intentionally never taught the floating girl.

"You don't want to though, right?" Her mother checked.

Of course she didn't. She wasn't stupid enough to think she'd be able to function on her own. She just wished they didn't make it so obvious that they knew it too. "No," she said. "But I want to start doing more. Skye's coming over or I'm going there again."

Her father sighed. "Just give us a heads up before she comes over."

"Thank you." She nodded.

The floating girl walked to her room.

She crawled under a weighted blanket and pulled out her phone.

Sadie: *I'm sorry I wasted your time today.*
Skye: *thanks for being so fun to waste time with :P*

She pulled the blanket a bit higher.

Skye: *serious though. it was nice, no need to apologize*

Her heart fluttered.

Sadie: *My parents said you could come over sometime soon.*
Sadie: *If you still wanted to.*

Skye: *hell yeah! let me know when*

She pulled her phone to her chest, smiled at her ceiling, and let her blanket hold her down.

The floating girl snuck out again that night. She slipped through the back door with a phone in her fist and a plan in her heart. She was going to figure this out. She'd finally learn how to stay on the ground and then she'd march right up to Skye Eaton and take her hand in hers without even having to consider any of the risks.

She walked to the middle of the forest, put her earbuds in, and pressed play.

Music was a common suggestion. At least two thirds of her therapists had mentioned it, but exactly none of her therapists had known the real reason that the floating girl needed to figure out how to keep herself calm. Music was supposed to be affective, and affect never went well for the floating girl. She turned up the volume, squeezed her eyes shut, and let herself drift up to the trees.

Then, she yelled. First just sounds then words then sentence. She even tried to pretend that she was yelling at someone. She tried trigger phrases and nonsense and every sound she could think of, but the floating girl remained frozen against the night sky.

Skye

"You're disgustingly happy this week," Isaac slipped in beside her at their cafeteria table on Monday.

"Shut up."

"You and your internet girlfriend finally make it official?"

She rolled her eyes. "I already told you we were going out."

"Right, but that's not official. And you're like, extra suspiciously happy this week."

Her cheeks flamed. She looked down to try and hide it. "Shut up," she mumbled.

"Are we talking about the O'Brian girl?" Kyle asked, hopping onto the chair beside Isaac. "Skye's all mushy and adorable again."

She kicked him under the table hard enough to make him yelp, but then he just laughed.

"We are then."

They were the type of friend group who told each other about every single date they'd ever been on, just for the sake of reminding each other that they were datable. Hearing her friends talk at length about their crushes had been a big part of Skye figuring out that she didn't like people in the same way they did. But she had no idea how to explain that Sadie had come over that Saturday without also explaining why none of them could meet her in person. Plus, she was pretty sure it hadn't technically been a date. It was a not-experiment that ended in watching movies together. Movies didn't have to inherently be romantic.

"I think they're official now," Isaac revealed.

"We're not."

"Okay." Kyle shrugged. "We'll just ask her tomorrow."

"Over your own dead bodies."

He laughed.

She knew he was just being an asshole (Kyle was in a constant state of being an asshole) but she was still extra on edge for their next sham book club meeting. She sat on the opposite side of their usual meeting table, as if that would help. Everyone's focus was always on Sadie anyway because she was the only one who ever had any idea what they were talking about. Skye read the books too, of course. That way she could slip her friends cues and questions to make the whole operation seem more legitimate to Ms. Rivera. Sadie'd offered to write up the questions for her to save her time, but even if Skye didn't really care about the books themselves, she liked actually being able to understand Sadie's impassioned analyses of them.

Mercifully, her friends stayed on task for the entire hour. They were sometimes the worst, but they were loyal where is counted. So, when Ms. Rivera asked her to stay behind after the meeting, she was confused.

"I've noticed our numbers are still down," Ms. Rivera said after the last of them (Trevor, parting salute at and all) had left.

Skye nodded. "I think we do fine as a small group. Don't you?"

Ms. Rivera sighed. "A public outreach club is supposed to include the public, Skye. Not just your friend group."

"I can't force anyone to join."

"I haven't seen it advertised anywhere."

Skye picked at her thumb. "I think it works better with a small group. Sadie's not really a people person." It wouldn't have even be a lie if she wasn't sure that Sadie would probably do better with most people than she would. "Wouldn't want to overwhelm her."

Ms. Rivera adjusted her glasses. "You can meet and chat with your friends without it being an official club. I don't see why—"

"We'll do the posters," she interrupted. She hadn't poured a month into this just to let another teacher think she was a disappointment. "and I'll email the announcement people tonight."

Ms. Rivera smiled. "Hopefully everyone's Fridays aren't all filled up yet."

Skye knew it wasn't a threat, but she couldn't help but hear it as one. She didn't have time to dwell on that though. She had a superpowered girl to go visit.

Skye was a bit over attached to her bike. When you didn't have your own car in a town too small to necessitate a public transit system, it was hard not to be. Normally when she rode it to friends' places she'd leave it in a garage she already knew the code to or throw it over a fence, but she hadn't thought to ask Sadie what her parents would want her to do and didn't want to make an even worse impression. If Skye had things her way, she wouldn't meet them at all.

She hated them a little, even though she knew that that wasn't fair. There was really no right way to deal with a child who could float away from you. But they'd made her feel like she was crazy when she was younger then spent years keeping Sadie away from her after that, so they were easy to hate.

The universe hated Skye though, so when she rang the bell, she was greeted by the same man who'd turned her away all those years ago.

"Hi," she smiled. She wiped her hand against her jeans before holding it out even though it wasn't dirty. Something about meeting Sadie's parents had her worried that she'd abruptly and miraculously become covered in mud. "I'm—"

"Skye," he finished for her. "You owe us a birdbath topper."

She laughed awkwardly, reminding herself to text Sadie next time to make sure she'd beat her parents to the door.

She almost reminded him that that wouldn't have happened in the first place if he hadn't decided to gaslight an elementary schooler, but she bit down on her tongue. She needed this to work. "Sorry about that," she said instead. "But you know, kids will be kids and all that."

"Skye!"

She let her shoulders relax when she saw Sadie rushing down the stairs to save her. She was in a dress again, this one light blue and paired with black leggings. She had thought the wardrobe choice was to allow for her to load her pockets with as many heavy things as possible, but apparently Sadie was just the kind of person who wore dresses in the fall. It would have been a confusing thing to realize about anyone else, but on her, it made perfect sense.

Sadie froze a foot away, hand already halfway to Skye's. She looked down at her feet and verified that they were still on the ground before letting her arm fall.

"We're going up to my room," Sadie told her father before turning back around and rushing up the stairs. Skye took off her shoes and followed.

Sadie's room looked exactly like her. The walls were each a different shade of pastel (blue, pink, yellow, and purple) and it was covered in nerd shit and every piece of Disney memorabilia imaginable. She had posters of Tinkerbell hung up right beside paintings of sharp-clawed fairies who looked ready to tear out something's throat and terrifying monster figurines lined up on the windowsill beside her stuffed animals as if everything fit together naturally because to Sadie, it probably did. Her bed was pink neat and covered by an actual canopy.

Skye pointed up at it, sitting down on the mattress. "Cool bed."

Sadie watched her for a moment, head tilted. "Was that serious or sarcastic?"

"Serious. Six-year-old me would have committed actual crimes for it."

"It's kid-ish."

"Yeah, and if they made grown-up sized race car beds, I'd have one right now. It's awesome."

"It's protective measures. I normally bump into something then stop raising so hitting the bottom's better than accidentally bumping into the light."

"Makes sense."

Sadie smiled a bit. "It's also kind of an excuse to have a really cool fairy tale bed."

Skye laughed. "Your dad hates me, by the way."

She rolled her eyes. "He doesn't hate you."

"He brought up me breaking your birdbath."

"Well," Sadie's eyebrows scrunched together. "you did."

"Accidentally!" She protested. "And when I was like, nine. Nothing people do before hitting double digits should count."

"He's just protective. Your school told him you were bullying me."

"Yeah, but I wasn't." She sat up a little straighter, watching Sadie carefully. "You know that, right? I just thought you were interesting as fuck and didn't know how to mind my own business."

She nodded, so Skye relaxed again. "We need to make sure you get the door next time. He might try to kill me if you leave me alone with him too long."

Sadie frowned. "He wouldn't—"

"Kidding," Skye stopped her. "Kind of."

"I was going to make sure I got it, for the record. I just thought you'd be here closer to the meeting ending and then I was umm... unavailable."

Skye frowned. "I freaked you out."

"Barely. sometimes I only need to get slightly worried for it to happen and I'm pretty much paranoid about everything all the time so—"

Skye grabbed her backpack from beside the bed. "I stopped at my mom's for snacks," she held out the Tupperware container. "Sorry, I'm just usually used to my friends being used to me doing that, I guess. I'll let you know next time. Or skip the stop and just bring smaller things like we used to."

Sadie sucked on her lip. "Is that what we are?"

"What?"

"You said friends. Is that... are we that?"

"Yes?" Skye decided. "And also more than that still, hopefully?"

"Okay," Sadie smiled. "Good. Thought I'd check."

"Didn't we already establish that?"

"I just wasn't sure..." she watched at her socks. "I can't touch you. Or look at you straight on."

"Right, which we've already established I'm fine with."

"Couples kiss."

"Some of them," Skye shrugged. "Eventually. But that's not like, a super important part of it for me? I'm not sure if it's the ace thing or just a me thing, but I'm fine with or without."

"Okay." She nodded. "Cool."

"Do your parents know?" Skye dropped her voice. "That you like girls?"

"I think maybe? They don't know it's you yet though. I mean, I think they suspect but..."

"Right." Skye nodded. "Have to trick them into liking me first. Good to know."

"What do we do now that you're here?" Sadie asked.

Skye shrugged. "It's your house."

"Right," she said quickly. "Right, yeah. I just didn't—right."

"We can watch more movies," Skye suggested. "Or play cards or a board game or something. Or just talk. I still have all my school stuff so we could always just work on our own stuff like we do on Skype?"

Sadie was the kind of person you could see thinking. It was like her eyes were tracking her thoughts. "Would it be weird to do that last one?"

Skye shrugged. "Not sure. It'd definitely make me a lot more likely to pass my test this Friday though."

Sadie nodded. "That then. For now."

Sadie took the desk, so Skye picked a section of floor to lie down on to get to work. They only got thirty minutes in before Sadie abruptly slammed her laptop shut and got up.

"I think we need to hold hands."

Sadie

There was once a floating girl who was extremely sure that this was an awful idea.

"You're sure this is a good idea?" Skye asked.

"Yes," the floating girl lied.

"I'm seriously fine with not doing that."

"I know," the floating girl lied.

"You're absolutely sure?"

"Yes," the floating girl lied. Her feet were already off the floor.

Skye sighed. "Sadie. You're nervous."

"Or excited," she said. "It also happens when I'm excited."

"Sadie."

"I'm already floating," the floating girl pointed out. "It can't make it worse. You might actually pull me down."

She rolled her eyes. "Fine."

The floating girl was already high enough that Skye had to reach up to grab her hand.

Hers was soft. It made sense, the floating girl knew that Skye didn't regularly partake in gymnastics or hard labour. But every time she'd read about people holding hands for the first time, one of them was always rough and the floating girl's hand was definitely also smooth. She wondered if that was what made her palm feel so hot. If opposite hands somehow negated the heat. She didn't know how anyone could keep holding on to something this warm.

Except she could. Because even as she pushed higher, Sadie couldn't manage to let go.

"You're freaking out."

She looked down. She'd gone high enough to pull Skye a few inches off the ground as well. Luckily, the ceiling met her before she could go much further.

"Good freaking out," she said. "This is good freaking out." It was. It was stomach spinning and head whirling, nausea inducing and toe curling, but it was definitely the good kind of freaking out. But Skye was still staring at her.

"It doesn't look like good."

The floating girl shook her head. "I told you. It happens when I'm happy too."

Skye let go. "You're all... frozen. That doesn't seem happy. I told you I'm fine with not—"

"I'm fine." The floating girl smiled. It was the most universal way to show someone that you were happy—unless you were an ape. Skye wasn't, but she kept frowning.

"We're not doing that again until you actually want to."

"I do!"

"You're freaking out Sadie."

The floating girl checked herself, but she was doing everything right. She was calm and breathing and smiling. She even felt herself start to come down a bit, now that the excitement of holding Skye's hand was wearing off.

"You don't get to tell me how I'm feeling," she argued.

Skye crossed her arms. "You keep closing your eyes and taking these massive, obvious breaths. That's clearly not fine."

"Oh," the floating girl relaxed fully. She finished her descent. "That's just how I calm down."

"If me touching you is something you need to calm down from, I don't want to keep doing it."

The floating girl frowned. "That's not fair. I told you what happens when I get overwhelmed. You knew—"

"I didn't know I was supposed to be fine with making you do fucking breathing exercises!"

"I'm not—"

Skye sighed, rushing to repack her bag. "I should go."

"Wait, you just—"

"Me being here is clearly not a good thing for you."

"It is!" The floating girl protested.

Skye kept packing.

"I don't want you to leave!"

Skye sighed again, pausing in the door. "I like you, I like being around you, but I'm not doing that if I have to feel like shit every time it happens."

"I wasn't trying to make you feel like shit!"

She knew she was rising again before it happened. She watched Skye's eyes follow her up.

"I know," she said. "We can... I don't know. We'll video chat, okay?"

And then she was walking down the stairs and the floating girl couldn't even chase after her.

Skye

Skye was a dick. Knowing that didn't make her any less of a dick. Maybe it made her an even bigger one.

She was a dick who'd left the girl she liked floating on her ceiling. She was a dick who made that girl turn into a statue the moment she touched her. She'd known that she couldn't touch Sadie. She'd been fine with that. But she hadn't signed up to have her beg her to do it anyway then freeze in disgust while trying to fight off a panic attack.

Skye was a dick, but she wasn't stupid. She'd grown up the token lesbian, and she couldn't even get that right. She was not the kind of lesbian that assholes swore that they could turn. She was too rude and too big and too unfocused on clothes and makeup for that. No, Skye was the kind of lesbian that made those assholes wrap a protective arm around their girlfriends while glaring at her across the hallway.

There was one universal rule all lesbians (especially her kind of lesbians) knew. Never make the "straight" girl uncomfortable. Even if she was the one who pulled you behind your cabin at sleep away camp and shoved her tongue down your throat. Even if she was the one who insisted you really did have to kiss in spin the bottle. If she was ever uncomfortable around you, if she ever decided to regret anything, it would always be your fault.

Skye knew that it wasn't that, with Sadie. Nothing was ever that simple with Sadie. But she still felt like she'd broken one of her most important rules so, like a dick, she ran. She ran home and tried to throw herself into studying and then when even that made her think of her, she sent an SOS text to the group chat to summon everyone available to Isaac's. Isaac's basement was always available, even if Isaac wasn't. She'd somehow talked her parents into giving Skye the spare key.

Only Isaac and Avan could make it. Neither of of them asked why she'd summoned them, and she didn't tell them because they already knew. They played Risk because it was the closest and longest game available, and nobody even hinted at Sadie's existence until Skye was leaving.

"Your fault or hers?" Isaac followed her to the door to ask. There was no need to specify. She already knew that there was only one other 'her' in Skye's life.

Skye sighed. "I don't know." Except she did know that it wasn't Sadie's. That didn't leave her with a lot of options. "Mine, probably."

"Fix it."

She rolled her eyes, turning to go.

"Skye," she caught her shoulder. "Fix it."

She rolled her eyes again and didn't respond, but she was going to fix it. Everyone listened to Isaac. That was just how she worked.

Sadie

There was once a girl in a bubble.

The problem was that her bubble, like most bubbles, was clear. The problem was that her bubble, unlike most bubbles, reflected so little light that you wouldn't know it existed until you'd already bumped into it.

The girl was fairly certain that she was the only person in the world born inside a bubble, though it was an impossible theory to test. Bubble people did not talk about being bubble people. It was one of the most important parts of being one. So, as a rule, the bubble girl only talked to people who could never get close enough to accidentally brush against her bubble's edges.

There were four friends in America, across four different states. Three in the UK. One in Australia and two in Asia. It was important for people to socialize, even if they lived inside bubbles, so her parents had always made sure that she had people to talk to--after running the best background checks normal civilians could, of course.

The problem was, they didn't know that she was a bubble person. She'd invented worlds for them---entirely different ones each time. She was going to be a writer and it felt like a good way to practice. In some she was popular. In some she was a wallflower. She was an athlete and mathlete and cheerleader and theatre kid. She was even a loner, to one, but the kind of loner who got up every morning and went to school just like the rest of them.

There was also an eleventh friend. A secret friend. One who'd required no background check to prove she was actually another child because she'd annoyed the bubble girl's parents in the way only a precocious preteen could. The only one she didn't feed made up stories because early on, the bubble girl had known that she'd wanted her to be different. She'd been certain that she'd wanted her to be real.

And so, the eleventh friend entered all ten fake stories. She was sometimes a rival and sometimes a best friend and a lot of the time something more. And her friends—in America and Europe and Asian and Australia—believed in every version of the eleventh friend. Maybe she'd become so real to them that the bubble girl had accidentally tricked herself too. Why else would she be naïve enough to try and pull her into the eleventh story?

When people run from you and you don't know why, you're supposed to ask your friends for advice. But the bubble girl did know why. It was the piece she'd left out of every other version of their story. The other girl had gotten close, reached for her, and was met with only soap.

There was no explaining that. Not after almost a decade of lies.

So, the girl and her bubble floated away from eleven reality-tinged tragedies as she tried to dream up a twelfth one instead.

It seemed no matter how many times she started one, she always forgot. All fairy tales—all real ones, anyway. All the ones that mattered most—ended in disaster.

Skye

Sadie: You left your container.
Sadie: It's too big for the hole. I can leave it on the porch
if you want. Just let me know when you're coming.
Sadie: I'm sorry.

If there was one thing Skye Eaton was supposed to be good at, it was apologizing. She'd been forced to pretend to do it so many times growing up that she considered herself an expert. She owned up to her mistakes instantly, immediately, and clearly.

She left Sadie on read until Friday. She kept almost responding, but she never went through with it. Finally, she didn't give herself space to keep fucking up. She gave each of her friends specific instructions on when and how to drag her over to Sadie's the next day if she didn't check in that night to tell them that she'd already stopped by on her own.

When she knocked on the door, Mr. O'Brian answered it again. She'd been expecting it this time. Sadie couldn't have known that she was coming.

"Hi," she started. "I—"

Mr. O'Brian closed the door in her face. He opened it again a few seconds later.

"Here." He held out an empty container. "Sadie said to give this to you."

"Is she home?" Skye tried to look past him. It was a stupid question. Sadie was almost always home.

"You shouldn't come in."

"Did she tell you that?"

He squinted at her. It was how Skye knew that she hadn't.

"Can you ask her for me?"

He sighed. "I don't think that's a good idea."

"Yeah, well that's up to her, isn't it?"

His eyes widened again. It was how Skye knew she'd fucked up, but she didn't particularly care. "I'll let her know—" He put an arm out to close the door again. This time, she pushed past it.

"Sadie!" She jogged up the stairs, hoping she hadn't misremembered the way to her room.

She heard Mr. O'Brian following her, so she sped up.

"Sadie." She knocked on her door when she found it closed. "Can I come in or do you want me to leave?"

"I already told her—" Sadie's father started to protest from behind her. Skye whipped around to face him.

"And I told you I was asking her. She's seventeen, not seven. Sadie!" She called again.

Finally, voice small, she responded. "Stay."

Skye stared at Mr. O'Brian, daring him to challenge her. He stared back. After a few tense seconds, he sighed. "At least take off your shoes."

Skye glanced down at her damp sneakers and blushed. "Right. Sorry." She pulled them off, handed them to him, and watched him begrudgingly disappear down the stairs. She knocked on the door again.

"Can I come in?"

"Yes!"

Skye sighed when she opened the door and found Sadie bobbing against her ceiling. She was an asshole. It occurred to her that over the course of just a couple of weeks she'd gone from seeing her maybe-girlfriend flying as world-altering to just another sign of her assholeness.

"I suck," she said, closing the door behind her.

"No, you don't," Sadie lied.

Skye took off her bag and sat down against the door.

"I was here a few days ago and you were fine. Now I show up and you go all the way to the ceiling."

"I'll come down eventually."

She sighed. "That's not the point, Sadie."

She watched her alternate between closing her eyes and whispering under her breath.

"Tell me the one about the tailor who fucks with the royals."

Sadie frowned. "There are a lot of those."

"Your favourite one then."

She nodded once, closed her eyes, and began. "There was once a princess..."

Skye leaned back and listened. By the time the story was finished, Sadie was back on the ground, eyes still closed.

"You're on the floor now." Skye tried to keep her voice quiet. She didn't know how little it would take for her to go drifting back up again.

"I know," Sadie said. "I think... I just need a minute."

Skye nodded, forgetting that she couldn't see her. She waited for her to slowly open her eyes and look at something just over Skye's shoulder.

"You came back," Sadie smiled a little.

Guilt tugged at her chest. "I should have right away."

"That's okay. Better late than never."

Skye frowned. "You can get mad at me, you know."

"But I'm not."

That didn't make sense to her. Sometimes Skye woke up mad at the rest of the universe just for existing. But she'd never known Sadie to lie, so she just nodded. "I shouldn't have ignored your texts. That was shitty."

"Yeah," Sadie admitted.

"I'm normally..." she tilted her head back against the door. "I'm good at apologies, for the record. I'm fucking fantastic at them with everyone else. You're just..."

"Too different?"

"Too overwhelming," she made herself look back at her. "Like, if I had very cool not-superpowers? I'd be all the way to the moon by now. I still don't know if I'm more terrified that you'll decide you still like me or that you never want to see me again."

"I would like to keep being girlfriends."

Skye forgot to make sure she didn't sigh out loud.

"Oh." Sadie tilted her head. "You don't."

"I like you so much it disgusts me," she admitted. If it took her three days to own up to anything, she owned her owning up to everything now. "But you looked fucking terrified, Sadie."

"I wasn't. That's just how—"

"I know, but it doesn't make it suck any less. We can... we can still be girlfriends. But it'd need to be like, an in name only thing because I don't think I'm ever going to be comfortable intentionally doing things we both know are going to freak you out."

She was quiet.

"Sadie? Would that be okay?"

"I want to be normal." Her voice trembled as she spoke. She pulled her knees up against her chest and wrapped her arms around them. "I want to do normal couple things."

Skye sighed. "I know. I want to be able to give you that but—"

"No!" Her feet came off the ground and Skye was convinced she was about to float back up again, but then they came down and she realized that she'd just started swaying. "That's not fair! You don't have to... you obviously don't have to... I'm going to figure out how to stop it! And then we can do normal things and go on normal dates and..."

"Sadie." Skye stopped her. "You're crying."

She laughed a little, wiping at her face. "Yeah, I noticed."

"No, I mean... shouldn't something be happening right now?"

Sadie froze. She stared up at the very distant ceiling. "Oh my god."

Sadie

There was once a girl with tears on her cheeks and two feet on the ground.

"Is this normal?" Skye Eaton asked her. "Has this happened before?"

"I'm—" She blinked. Tilted her head to the side to get her brain in the perfect position. "I don't think so. Or... sometimes maybe, but only when I'm alone." She didn't have to check her pulse to know that she was not supposed to be on the ground.

"Okay," Skye stood up. "That's good, right? It's another clue. Are you... mad right now? Or a few seconds ago?"

"Of course not," she said instantly. "It's not your fault."

"Okay." Skye repeated. "So it's not an anger specific thing. What are you feeling right now? Or a few seconds ago, I mean."

"Upset?" She guessed. "Frustrated?"

Skye was looking at her too intently for comfort, but every time the floating girl tried to tell her that, her tongue started to tangle. She shut her eyes. Counted to three.

"What was that?"

"What?"

"Just now. What's wrong?"

She froze. Skye had been looking at her too intently, so of course she'd caught it. The floating girl needed to choose a new calming strategy. This one made Skye Eaton run away.

"Shit," Skye said.

The floating girl was leaving the ground again.

"Sorry. Obviously I wasn't supposed to point it out. Let me umm..." she turned around to face the door. "Is this better? Worse?"

The floating girl let out a long breath. As the air escaped her, the rest of her followed it back down. "Better."

"Okay. You said it's happened before, right? What were you doing then? How were you feeling?"

"I don't know," the floating girl lied. It was always dark when it happened. She was always small. Always shaking. Sometimes in corners or under blankets or in closets, tasting salt on her trembling lips. "Sad? I guess?"

"Were you crying then too?"

"I think so," she lied again. "Yes."

Skye was quiet. "I have a theory. Can I do something that'll freak you out on purpose?"

"I'm... okay. Yes."

It didn't matter. The floating girl already felt her pulse picking up. She'd be in the air soon whether by Skye Eaton's hand or her own. "You're fine when you yell when you're angry and when you cry when you're upset, right? I'm going to take your hand. I need you to do whatever being... whatever emotion that gives you makes you want to do."

Her pulse slowed again. It was too simple of a theory. If it was that easy, she would have figured it out years ago. Yes, the floating girl had stayed grounded while crying a handful of times, but it was far more likely to make her airborne. She craved a too hot hand though, so she didn't point that out.

Skye turned back around and took her hand. It made the floating girl happy. It made her a million other tiny things too—so many tiny things that she didn't know how one body could possibly be containing that many emotions all at once—but happiness was the easiest to name and the easiest to express. She tensed the muscles in her cheek. She smiled. It did not stop her from being pulled up.

Skye sighed, letting go of the floating girl far too quickly.

"Sorry," she said. She didn't turn around, but she still tilted her head down towards the carpet. Maybe she knew more than the floating girl had realized. "Guess it's not that."

"I knew it wouldn't work," the floating girl admitted. "I should have warned you. Thanks for trying."

"We'll figure it out," Skye said. "For real, eventually. We must be getting close to something. But for now, I can't..."

"I can deal with liking you without being able to make physical contact."

Skye smiled slightly. "Yeah?"

The floating girl made herself shrug. "I managed for four years, right? It'll be easy."

Except it wasn't. Maybe that was part of her curse. It was infinitely more difficult to accept that she'd never be able to touch Skye Eaton now that she was physically within arm's reach. So, even though Skye's theory had made no sense, it was all she thought about all weekend. That Sunday, the floating girl climbed out of bed, put in her earbuds, and pressed play.

Music rarely caused one distinct emotional response. It was a hurricane of euphoria and longing and excitement and sadness. Unlike holding hands with a pretty girl though, the floating girl knew exactly what kind of bodily response it was supposed to elicit.

She did not know how to dance. It was a hard thing to learn when your feet could never be on the ground while music was playing loudly enough for one to actually pay it the attention and focus required for dancing. But as she slowly drifted towards the ceiling, the floating girl tried to mimic every style she'd ever heard of. She pressed her hands against the ceiling in mock pirouettes. She tapped her feet against an unreachable floor. She cycled through every dance move—both professional and otherwise—she could think of, but she remained suspended in the air. It was only when she gave up—when failed attempts at grace were traded for nonsensical swaying and shaking and waving—that her feet became reacquainted with the ground.

The floating girl flew to her phone.

Guess where I am right now? She texted Skye.

Except it was 3am so even though the floating girl was suddenly full of so much energy that she had to hop in place to keep from celebrating aloud and waking her parents, Skye was probably asleep like the rest of the world.

On the ground. She answered for her.

Then, grinning so wide she was certain that her face would split, she climbed back into bed and pretended to try and fall asleep.

Skye

Skye got a B+.

It wasn't a world ending disaster. The test was worth next to nothing so it should have meant absolutely nothing. Except Skye Eaton was not supposed to be the kind of person who got Bs.

It put her a shit mood made extra shitty since she knew that she'd have to be the biggest asshole on the planet to make her friends listen to her complain about something as insignificant as a B. It made her feel extra asshole-y when they all instantly caught on anyway.

"Be careful. Skye's about to kill someone," Avan mock-whispered in warning when Isaac finally showed up at their lunch table two minutes later than she normally did.

Skye rolled her eyes, not looking up from the practice test she was redoing as she shoved his shoulder. Luckily, it was muscle memory by that point.

"What happened?" Isaac asked, sitting down beside her.

"She probably got a 92 or something," Kyle guessed.

"79." She grumbled.

If they were going to be annoying, they could at least be annoying and accurate.

"Oh shit," Isaac said. "What happened?"

On cue, Skye's phone rang. She sighed, pushing the test away to answer it. She'd been the one to tell Sadie her lunch hour. It wasn't like she could just pretend to be busy.

"Hey Sadie," she tucked her phone against her ear so she could get back to work. "What's— hey!" She jumped out of her chair when Isaac pulled the phone free and held it to her own ear.

"Hey Sadie. Skye can't talk right now. She got an average grade so she'll need about 2-3 business days to spiral and recuperate."

Skye tried to snatch the phone back from Isaac, but she stepped around the table.

"No, she's fine, she just needs to ignore everyone for a bit until she decides she's back to be adequately over-prepared for everything. She hasn't figured out how to say no to you yet though so I need you to leave her alone for the next like 48ish hours, yeah? Cool. Thanks."

She handed the phone back to Skye.

"I hate you," she glared, already opening her texting app to send Sadie an apology.

Isaac rolled her eyes. "Someone has to protect us all from you inevitably exploding."

Skye pulled a piece of dead skin off of her lip. "Did she sound—"

"She said it was totally fine. And if it's not, now you get to blame me instead of feeling guilty about it yourself."

She kept glaring. Even as she put her phone away, picked up her pencil, and got back to work.

Skye was not naturally good at most things. She'd pretend she was, of course. If anyone tried to claim that she cared about anything, she would deny it to her grave. But every single thing Skye was good at had come from years of effort.

She'd only learned how to bake after years of burnt cookies and oversalted brownies and even then, she didn't think she would have been able to get a job at any bakery not owned by her own mother. She'd only learned how to lash out with words instead of fists after two black eyes, three sprained fingers, and six suspensions. She'd only learned it was important to get good grades after one particularly evil sixth grade teacher had finally reached her breaking point and demanded "what the hell do you think you're going to do with the rest of your life?"

Skye's only future plan had always been running away. When she was younger, it was because her town was boring. As she got older, it was because she realized that it was suffocating. Small towns were only cozy if you fit into them. If Skye had to stay, she knew that she'd struggle with that her entire life, queer or not. She was going to be a lesbian somewhere where she could be loud and proud and obnoxious about it one moment then go grab groceries without anyone knowing anything about her the next.

So, Skye had decided that she would have to be good at school. Bar winning the lottery, it seemed like the easiest way to get somewhere better. She learned to leave her phone downstairs with her parents the moment she got home and refused to retrieve it until she'd mastered everything she wanted to work on that night. She learned to live by cue cards and highlighters and study guides. It took years, but by the time she was seventeen, she had perfected it.

It should have been easy then, to go home and get caught back up. It should have taken a day tops. But instead, she found herself refreshing her email and wandering downstairs every thirty minutes to recheck her phone, just in case she'd missed another text from Sadie.

It had taken years, but Skye had finally mastered the art of running away. Except suddenly, she kept drifting towards her.

Sadie

There was once a girl whose writing was interrupted by a knock on the door.

The girl had read enough fairy tales to know that it was never wise to answer mysterious knocks, so she hesitated.

"Sadie," a voice—the voice she hadn't even realized that she was waiting for—said. "Can I come in?"

The girl opened the door. "It hasn't been forty-eight hours yet."

Skye rolled her eyes. "Isaac's a bitch."

"She just cares about you."

"I know. That's what makes her such a bitch. Your dad let me in." She sat down on the floating girl's bed. The floating girl was kind of obsessed with that. The way she acted like her presence in her bedroom was such a given that she'd plop herself down on her bed without a second thought. "He barely even protested this time. I think he's warming up to me."

The floating girl did not correct her.

"Have I been distracting you?" She asked. "From your schoolwork?"

Skye rolled her eyes again. The floating girl was getting better at reading her eyerolls. They almost always meant that she was about to say something untrue. "I got a B+. Literally only one percent away from an A. It's not the end of the world."

"I have been though, right? It was my fault?"

She sighed. "Sadie. I'd rather hang out with you than get an extra percent."

Sometimes, Skye answered questions by not answering them.

"You don't have to be here," the floating girl told her.

Skye shrugged. "You didn't talk in book club again today. I wanted—"

"That wasn't your fault. That just... happens, sometimes."

"I know," Skye frowned. "I just wanted to hear you talk. Or type or whatever, obviously you don't have to—I just wanted to hang out."

The floating girl hugged her chest. "I don't want to stress you out either."

"You're not—"

She checked her clock. "It's four fifteen."

"So?"

"You study for at least three hours a night before doing anything else. I know you didn't already study for one yet because we had a meeting and if you stay here for what? Two hours? That means you'll either get home at six thirty and not have dinner until almost ten or you're planning on messing up your whole schedule a day after you were apparently just freaking out about studying."

Skye frowned. "I don't... how did you—"

"We traded schedules in ninth grade, remember?"

Skye rolled her eyes. "That was ninth grade. I don't still—"

"When we video chat any time between three-thirty and six-thirty, you're always in the middle of working on something. You still do it."

Skye sighed. "Why'd you call yesterday?"

The floating girl hesitated. She hadn't even told her parents yet. She needed to tell someone, but that could wait until after she'd upheld her promise to go forty-eight hours without distracting her.

"I'll tell you tomorrow."

"Sadie."

"Tomorrow! Go home. Study."

"What if I do that here?"

The floating girl tilted her head to the side. "Fine," she decided. "I'll allow it. But only if you actually get work done. No using me to procrastinate."

Skye grinned. "Deal."

There was once a girl who was not going to float. Not that afternoon, at least. She would keep both feet pressed against the ground and prove that a few nights ago hadn't been a fluke.

She met Skye at her front door the next day and rushed her up to her bedroom. "I need to show you something," she declared.

"The Monday phone call thing?"

"The Monday phone call thing. You brought a speaker?"

Skye nodded, pulling it out of her backpack to hand it to her.

"I can't do music," she explained. "Or... not good music. I can do elevator music I guess but nothing actually worth listening to."

"Okay?"

The floating girl plugged in her phone, hit play, and waited to be taken up to the ceiling. Skye reached for the cord when she started floating, but she shook her head.

"Wait," she said. "I've got it."

She almost didn't. It was easy to nod and sway and shake when she'd been alone. It was harder to do so with an audience. Especially an audience she knew that she was supposed to be trying to impress.

"Sadie..." Skye started, reaching for the phone again.

"I said I've got it."

She danced. Horribly and awkward and spectacularly. She could feel Skye watching her as she descended so she squeezed her eyes shut and didn't risk opening them again until she was back on the ground.

Skye was smiling. Skye was laughing.

The floating girl scrambled to unplug the phone before she drifted back out of range.

"Sorry," she said. "That was probably weird. I don't know why... sorry."

Skye frowned. "I'm sorry, am I seriously supposed to pretend that you fucking dancing mid-air wasn't one of the coolest things I've ever seen?"

"You were laughing."

"Well, yeah. Because it looked fun. And kind of because you're a shit dancer but I am too so I don't really get to judge you for that. Mostly because it looked fun though, I promise. Very jealous I can't do that."

The floating girl shifted from foot to foot. "You could with me. If you want. If I hold on to you—"

"You won't be able to stay on the ground."

"Right, but that's kind of the point, right? If you want." She repeated. "I don't know what it feels like when I take anyone with me so if it hurts or anything—"

"It doesn't."

Skye Eaton held out her arms. The floating girl plugged her phone back in, pressed play, and took them.

It was not a fairy tale moment. It wasn't even a movie one. The music was too loud and too fast and too frantic, and they were holding each other more to keep themselves connected than for anything romantic as they twisted in the air, but it made the floating girl laugh until her lungs ached, so maybe that was better than any fairy tale moment could have been. Laughter—the happy kind, at least—was hard to come by in those.

The floating girl didn't know how long they danced or when she went from holding onto Skye Eaton because she had to to doing it simply because she could. She didn't even notice her mother crack the door open to stop the source of all the sound coming from her normally silent daughter's room only to quietly retreat and return with her father in tow before the two crept away together, suddenly a lot more forgiving of the girl who'd broke birdbaths and branches. Because at some point, both girls had returned to the ground.

Skye

"I held your hands today. Both of them."

Skye rolled her eyes then remembered that she was alone and let herself grin like an idiot.

"Yeah," she said, phone pressed between her cheek and the pillow. "You did. I was there."

She would admit it to no one (especially not her friends who definitely wouldn't consider hand holding gossip worthy) but she was pretty sure her heart was still skipping beats.

"I bet I could do it again too," Sadie said. "Next time you come over. Or I could probably come over there? Or we could probably even go somewhere else if—"

Skye's smile fell. "Sadie."

"Today was nice."

"It was," Skye said. "Really, really nice. But it worked under extremely controlled circumstances."

"It might work in public."

"What if it doesn't?"

Sadie was quiet.

"We're having a picnic," Skye decided right then and there.

She sighed. It made the line go staticky. "You don't have to—"

"No. Shut up. We're going to have a picnic on Sunday before it becomes too gross and cold to do one and I literally know for a fact you have no other plans, so you're not allowed to say no."

"Okay," she said. "What do I bring?"

Skye brought the blanket and basket and cookies and even tiny finger sandwiches that she'd stuck toothpicks through for added flourish. She told Sadie to show up at the park at noon so she got there at 11:45 so she could scope out an isolated spot close enough to the treeline for them to disappear into it if they had to.

The park was virtually empty (she'd chosen an unpopular one intentionally) but she wanted to have the option just in case.

She let Sadie be in charge of fruit and water. She knew that her parents had supposedly given up on all the weird diets they'd had her on as a kid once Sadie had finally convinced them that her floating wasn't the result of an iron shortage, but she didn't trust the picnic choices of someone who'd grown up thinking kale chips were a dessert.

When Sadie got there (exactly at noon) she smiled and waved so Skye smiled back, even though she was already beginning to worry. Sadie wore a blue checkered dress, a thin jacket, tights, and sneakers. Even if her dress did have pockets, she was clearly being a lot less cautious than she had been the last time they'd met outside when there hadn't even been people around. Skye glanced towards the trees.

"Hey!" Sadie sat down.

She reached to hug her but Skye flinched back.

She frowned. "Sorry, I didn't mean to—"

"You know it's not you," Skye stopped her. She looked pointedly at the elderly couple sitting on a bench a few feet away.

Sadie tilted her head to the side. "You're the one who said It'd be cool if people found out."

"It would be. But you clearly didn't agree and I'm not fucking that up for you."

"It'll be fine. I've been practicing. If I just get rid of the energy before it reaches my head, we're all good."

Skye made herself smile. "Let's not test it quite yet, yeah?"

Sadie nodded, sitting down. "I brought drinks and orange slices." She opened her purse and handed Skye a water bottle. She stared at the basket. "Which obviously wasn't enough."

Skye rolled her eyes. "I asked you out. I was supposed to do most of the work, that's how these things work." She opened the basket and started unpacking. "Plus, I work at a bakery in the summers. This is like, my one skill. I obviously had to show off."

"You made these?"

She nodded. "Even the finger sandwiches. We're an extremely anti-store bought family."

Sadie smiled. "I was always jealous of that, you know."

"My mom would absolutely hire you if I asked her to," Skye realized. "She needs more help during the school year anyways. I promise she won't snitch if she ever walks into the back and finds you on the ceiling."

Sadie's eyes widened. "I didn't mean... thanks, but baking's not really for me. I'm fine with cooking and stuff but touching raw dough's too freaky."

Skye had never been worried that her parents would be angry if she brought a girl home. How they'd react to one who didn't like baking was an entirely different story.

"I just meant the baker parent part," Sadie continued. "It's the perfect parent profession. In stories they're always the ones who want kids the most and take care of them the hardest."

Skye rolled her eyes, watching as Sadie picked apart a finger sandwich to pop the cucumber slice into her mouth. "I'm sure if business people were popular enough back then they all would have been like, obsessed with their kids."

"Yeah," she said. "Maybe."

"And that lady who makes the gingerbread man? I'm pretty sure she leads the mob trying to devour him."

"She's the exception to the rule then." She put the sandwich back together and chewed slowly. "I haven't told my parents yet. That I think we've figured out the floating thing."

Skye frowned. "Why wouldn't—"

"It just doesn't make sense? I've been experimenting more and it seems like it happens when I try to keep myself from showing emotions but that's everything we've been... my natural instinct is to try to stop from doing it which is what sends me up, right? But I only developed that instinct because I was already floating. Infants don't decide to just not cry."

Skye shrugged. "That's just more of a reason to tell them, right? Connect the pieces?"

"Yeah, I guess." She crossed her legs beneath her, swaying slightly with the wind. "I just don't want them to feel guilty? If they're part of the reason we couldn't figure out how to control it?"

"I mean, if they are, maybe they should feel guilty."

Her head shot up. "They're my parents."

"Right, and if they kept you locked away from everything for years when they didn't have to, that's a valid thing to be pissed about."

Sadie looked away from her again, fist tapping against the ground. Skye resisted the urge to point out that if they were going by fairy tale logic, the people who kept girls locked away in towers were rarely the good guys in those. She was pretty sure Sadie'd already realized that.

"I'm also... I don't want them to think I have it too under control? I do," she quickly added. "I think. I spent all day yesterday walking around and testing environments and emotions and I was fine, but it was also... really tiring? Which is weird, right? Because if I'm right and all I have to do is let my body do whatever it wants to when I get overwhelmed then it should have been more tiring supressing that but it feels like double the work right now? Like—" she held out a hand. "I'm finding that I like moving my wrist a lot if I'm excited or stressed or... pretty much anything I guess. The way I move it changes though. But I was walking over here and I was excited, obviously. You're very exciting and it's all very inconvenient for me."

Skye blushed at that, biting at her lip to try and lessen her reaction.

"But I was excited and the first thing my body wanted to do was make sure I didn't seem excited so I froze up then I felt myself rising and I had to remind myself to shake out my wrist and then I was hyperaware of shaking my wrist and it was kind of double the work? I'm fine and I can do stuff like this but I don't want them to get excited and think I'll finish off high school the normal way or anything. I'm pretty sure that'd still be too much for me."

"I'm sure they wouldn't pressure you into anything."

"I know, it's just..." she sighed. "It's a lot. Sorry, this is all... thank you. For helping me figure things out and the cookies and picnic. I didn't mean to..."

"I want to hear about your problems," Skye stopped her. "That just means I get to bombard you with mine."

She tilted her head. "Do you have any?"

"Well, there's this girl I'm obsessed with who apparently doesn't like baking."

Her eyes widened. "I can—"

Skye laughed. "Kidding. I'm a shit cook so it balances. I can handle all the baking." She thought for a minute. "Honestly though, I think my biggest problem right now is the whole graduating thing? Like, I've been counting down to it forever but it suddenly feels too close. I'm either going to not get into any of the programs I want—"

"You will."

She rolled her eyes. "Yeah, only because you make me look all introspective and responsible to Ms. Rivera, so thanks for that. But I either don't get in and all of this was for nothing or I do and move away from literally everyone I care about." Skye paused. "You could come visit all the time though, once we're more confident with the floating stuff. Or move out entirely? You can write from pretty much anywhere."

Sadie's fist pounded against the ground. Her swaying got slightly faster. "I don't think... Toronto sounds like a lot."

"Right, yeah. Eventually though. Isaac'd kill me if I agreed to live with anyone else, but we could have like, apartments in the same building. It would be fun."

"Sounds nice."

"But yeah. I guess I'm excited for change and terrified of it simultaneously. Never tell anyone I admitted this, but I'm gonna miss the shit out of my friends here."

She drew two fingers across her mouth. "My lips are sealed."

Skye snacked on ginger cookies while Sadie picked apart another sandwich.

"What if I meet them?" Sadie suddenly said.

"My friends? You've already met them all. I'm not actually that popular."

"In person though."

Skye hesitated.

"Don't do that. You're the one who acted like it was stupid to hide away."

"I know, but—"

"If you're trying to do what I want, I'm telling you I want to practice meeting people in person. If you trust your friends that's the smartest place to do it. Plus that's a normal thing couples do, right? Meet each other's friends?"

She swallowed. "Okay. Sure."

Sadie frowned. "Do you not want me too? I know we agreed to date when you didn't think I'd ever meet them in person, but if you're not comfortable with—"

"Sadie." She put a hand on her knee, just in case. She hadn't yet learned how to decipher between the early stages of swaying or floating. "My friends know about us. I'm just nervous, okay? You're like, the coolest thing about me."

Her forehead creased. "But you said you wouldn't... you didn't tell them about the floating, right?"

She rolled her eyes. "The single most boring thing about you? No. I haven't."

Sadie abruptly got up. "I'd like to kiss you. Can I?"

"I... what?" Skye faltered.

"Not as an experiment or test, I just want to do it because you're cool and pretty and stuff. Would that be okay?"

"I..." Skye blinked. Looked around. "Yes? Very yes? But maybe not when we're in public."

Sadie cocked her head to the side. "I've been in control all weekend. It'll be—"

"Maybe you're vastly underestimating how good of a kisser I am."

Sadie laughed. It wasn't fair because Skye was suddenly the one blushing, even though it had been her joke. She'd kissed three people her entire life. Presumably, Sadie had kissed none, but that just meant she'd expect Skye to be the better kisser.

Sadie held out a hand. "Come on. We'll go hide."

She was going to kiss a girl obsessed with happily ever afters in a forest. Like there was nothing intimidating about that.

They stood inches apart between the trees. "Ready?" Sadie asked.

Skye laughed. It felt so giddy and big and immature. Maybe it was. She'd heard queer people talking about hitting each awkward dating phase slightly later in life, but she hadn't thought that had applied to her because she'd never kissed a girl that had mattered. She was almost an adult, but maybe this was her coming of age. Maybe Sadie would taste like middle school.

"Wait," Skye said. She held out both of her hands.

Sadie stared at them. "I told you, I'm not going to float. No one can see us anyway. It's fine if I do."

"I know. But if you go up, I'm coming too."

She took her hands and shuffled further forward. "Ready?" she whispered again.

All Skye could do was nod.

Their lips touched. That was it. Skye abruptly realized that she'd never once actually initiated a kiss and vaguely remembered that there were sometimes tongues involved so she stuck hers out slightly, hit Sadie's lips, and then pulled away again. It was a lot more middle school than she'd been going for.

She felt Sadie's arms rise and worried they were about to be in the air, but when she opened her eyes, she was just hopping in place.

Skye winced. "Sorry. That was... less than romantic."

Sadie shrugged. "Then we'll just have to keep practicing."

Sadie

There was once a sometimes-floating girl, but that afternoon was not going to be one of those sometimes.

She had prepared for every possible hazard. She'd memorized each of Skye's friends' faces so she wouldn't get any of their names wrong and had verified where each of them normally sat as an extra precaution. She'd walked the route to Isaac's address twice even though Skye was going to walk it with her, just to make sure there weren't any surprises along the way. She'd gotten Skye to suggest an activity—monopoly: easy, long, and structured—and practiced both winning and losing online to make sure neither sensation would send her skyward. Learning earthly instincts was a hard task for a girl who'd grown up assuming she was destined for the sky, and no internet clues seemed to fit her quite right. Still, she learned that most of the time, when she lost, her knuckle liked to rap against her calf. When she won, her wrists and elbows—maybe remembering their skyward tendencies—liked to flap.

Skye did not do this. Neither did any of her friends, apparently, which Skye kept assuring her wouldn't be noticeable, but the sometimes-floating girl knew it was, because her parents had already noticed the change. They never brought it up directly though and she wasn't ready to, so they all pretended not to notice each other noticing. Anything less than calf rapping or arm flapping didn't consistently keep her grounded though, so it would have to do.

The sometimes-floating girl waited by the door for Skye to arrive. Her parents did not know where they were going and Skye did not know that her parents didn't know, so it would be best if she limited their interactions with each other. The sometimes-floating girl was seventeen. She was old enough to carry her own secrets.

"Hi." She had the door open before Skye could even knock, quickly slipping through it the moment it was wide enough for her to and closing it behind her.

"Hey!" Skye smiled. If she was suspicious, she didn't show it. "Ready to go?"

The sometimes-floating girl rolled her wrists then held out a hand.

She was brought to a basement. Floating girls were diametrically opposed to basements, but she was only a sometimes-floating girl now, so she allowed herself to be pulled underground. Someone whistled when they reached the bottom of the stairs. It was high and sharp and loud. She resisted the urge to pull her hands to her ears then resisted the urge to resist her urges and let go of Skye's hand to cover them.

"Hey," Skye addressed the group.

The sometimes-floating girl didn't know if they were staring at her because she was new or covering her ears or if she'd just started floating again and was the last to notice. She slowly lowered her hands.

"This is Sadie." Skye squeezed her wrist when it was back at her side.

"Hi, Sadie," the group monotoned in unison.

She tensed the muscles in her cheeks.

Skye started walking towards the couches, leaving her at the foot of the stairs. "Sade?" She turned around. "You coming?"

She took a deep breath, rolled her wrists, and followed.

Skye's friends were fascinating in person, but the floating girl couldn't properly appreciate that yet. They'd lived in her brain—and sometimes in her stories, in the ones where she'd written herself into their friend group—as archetypes for years. They were more complex in real life. She should have already known that. Archetypes didn't make much sense outside of books. They were loud and funny and so, so, clearly in love with each other, even though no one ever said it out loud. She would come back, she'd decided. If they'd have her. She'd learn how to rewrite them more accurately in her mind. But that first time meeting them, she was too focused on the world within her body to properly process anything beyond it.

Sometimes, the sometimes-floating girl's throat forgot that it belonged to her. Her parents called it shyness. Her therapists called it anxiety. It was more than that though. It was a battle, one always fought on its terms instead of the girl's. Sometimes it was predictable. She'd be upset or frustrated or actually shy or anxious and the disconnect would follow. Sometimes, she didn't know how or why it was going to happen until she was already in the middle of a war.

Sitting there on the couch, even though no one had said or done anything wrong, she felt her words start to freeze. It happened just at her collarbones. The words and air and intent got that high until they refused to move past whatever invisible barricade her throat had put up. Sometimes, she could corral them together. Sometimes, if she pushed enough words up, a few would break through. But it required almost all of her focus and energy so most of the time, she just waited for her throat to decide that she was no longer a threat.

She was not oblivious enough to think they hadn't noticed when she'd gone from buying and selling properties out loud to wordlessly pointing at cards and handing over fake money. Skye had pulled out her phone when she'd first gone silent, but she'd shaken her head and pushed it back towards her pocket. Typing was much more noticeable than silence.

The problem with going silent around people was that knowing that they'd that noticed—knowing that they knew that girls did not normally go to battle with their own muscles—rarely helped. She spent that first hour so distracted with trying to talk and trying to ignore everyone ignoring the fact that she couldn't that she didn't even process she was winning until the game was already nearing its end. Still, ongoing battle or not, nothing could distract her enough to keep her from celebrating the sweet taste of victory. Her arms tried to fly but the rest of her did not so no body stared at her strangely as they cleaned up the game. Skye leaned towards her while a pair of her friends went to put it away. "Want to leave?" She whispered.

The floating girl shook her head. She might not have been able to talk, but she could still listen. She wanted to see how Skye's world looked.

Skye leaned back against the couch and pulled her legs up with her, watching her friends talk about their days. The sometimes-floating girl caught bits of pieces. When she didn't Skye would lean towards her to connect the dots.

"Avan hates Ms. Delousy."

Or

"Kyle's madly in love with her, he just hasn't admitted it yet."

Even though she knew the sometimes-floating girl wouldn't contribute anything. Maybe because the sometimes-floating girl couldn't contribute anything. They directed jokes and facts and anecdotes towards her, but never questions. Slowly, it stopped feeling like they were avoiding it because they'd noticed something about her and more like they were all falling into a routine they'd somehow already known. No one was asking her questions so when her throat finally came unstuck again, she decided to ask one of her own.

"I like your laptop," she pointed at Trevor's. "What are the stickers from?"

Everyone froze for an almost imperceivable second before getting back to talking. She realized she hadn't thought to check if she was interrupting something. Her fist hit her calf.

"My friend makes them," Trevor said. "They're mostly OCs."

"Cool."

Avan groaned. "Trevor has like four separate cooler friend groups than ours. Don't give him any more reasons to run away."

Trevor nodded solemnly. "It's true. I'm the popular one."

"He's full of shit," Skye informed her. "None of us are the popular one. It's why we work. He has to play D&D with people from the catholic school and the internet because everyone here sucks."

The sometimes-floating girl nodded. "I have a friend who plays dungeons and dragons. She makes it sound like fun."

Everyone froze, staring at Trevor.

Skye pointed a finger in his face. "No kidnapping my very cool girlfriend to do nerd shit multiple nights a week."

Trevor frowned. "What about once a week?"

She considered. "I suppose I'll allow it."

Trevor grinned, leaning towards the sometimes-floating girl. "Okay. So if you wanted to join, my online group is starting a new campaign on Wednesdays soon? It's actually not as hard to pick up on as it seems and it's like... you like stories, right? It's basically just stories but collaborative and with dice and shit. It's actually perfect timing, it'd definitely be the best one for you to join. It's all online so perfect for people who umm..." he paused, looking to Skye. "Are homeschooled?" He guessed. "My cousin runs it so like half the group's autistic too."

The sometimes-floating girl froze.

Skye reached across the coffee table to smack his knee. "Shut up, don't be—" She stopped mid sentence, pressing a hand down against the sometimes-floating girl's lap.

Because the sometimes-floating girl had froze.

She quickly tried to get her body back to natural unnaturally, standing up to try and explain away any early signs of floating anyone else might have caught on to. Luckily for her, most non-floating people had become so convinced that magic wasn't real, that their brains had mastered explaining it away.

Everyone was watching her.

"Bathroom's to the left," Isaac said. "If you needed it."

Everyone was watching her.

"You okay?" Skye checked.

"Yeah." She looked down at her feet then remembered that normal people didn't look down at their feet to check if they were okay then remembered that she should have let herself anyway when she felt her heels start to rise. The sometimes-floating girl didn't know if she was worse at being normal or being herself. "Just have to use the bathroom. I'll be back."

She speed-walked the whole way there and slammed the door shut behind her, just in case she couldn't ground herself in time.

Skye

"Skye..."

"Shut up." She ignored Trevor, hastily packing up her remaining cookies and containers. There was no way Sadie was going to want to stay.

"No one was trying to upset her!"

She stopped to glare at him. She'd planned this perfectly. She'd debriefed everyone on exactly what they could and couldn't say and he'd still fucked it all up.

"You weren't supposed to bring up her not leaving the house," she simmered.

"That's kind of an unavoidable part of inviting someone to join an online campaign. I just—"

"And not only did you bring it up, but you decided to make fun of her in the same sentence? What the fuck!"

She was extremely aware of Avan and Kyle slowly creeping back upstairs. Cowards.

"Skye." Isaac grabbed her elbow, trying to calm her down.

She shook herself free. "Can you go ask her if she wants to leave? Tell her I'm all good to go if she is."

She hesitated, but left.

"You—" she whirled around on Trevor again, fist shaking. He caught her arm.

"It's not bullying to call a homeschooled person homeschooled."

"You didn't... you fucking called her autistic! She doesn't get it when people are jokingly mean sometimes. I told you—"

"Yeah, I know she doesn't. Probably because of the autism?"

Skye froze. "I... what?"

"My cousin Manny's autistic and so are most of his friends? Which you'd know if you ever made time to play with us, by the way." He sighed. "I'm sorry, I didn't know you didn't

know. I figured if you felt the need to debrief us on all of Sadie's—
"

"Sadie's not autistic."

He nodded. "Okay, cool. I shouldn't have said anything."

"Why did you think she was?"

He sighed, running a hand through his air. "Skye, I literally just told you I have multiple autistic friends. Being all defensive over the fact that I thought your girlfriend might be is kind of a dick move."

"No, I didn't..." she squeezed her fist. "That's obviously not a problem. I just don't know why you thought—" she stopped herself. She did know. But it wasn't because Sadie was autistic, it was because she had secret superpowers.

Trevor sighed again. "If she hasn't said anything about it I probably shouldn't. Tell her I didn't mean anything by it, yeah?"

He tried to leave, but she caught his arm. "If she does is it like... is it creepy or exploitative if I'm dating her?" She knew that Sadie wasn't autistic, but if she seemed like she was, it still felt like an important thing to check.

His eyes narrowed. "You're asking me if it's creepy for you, a seventeen-year-old lesbian, to date a seventeen-year-old girl?"

"But if she's autistic—"

"I didn't say I thought she was mentally slow. Jesus Christ, Skye. She's just spent over an hour kicking all of our collective asses at a board game."

Isaac waved from the top of the stairs, giving them a thumbs up. "She says she's good to go."

Skye sighed. "That's my cue."

This time when she tried to leave, Trevor was the one to pull her back. "Promise me you're not about to go treat your girlfriend like a toddler because of something I said."

"Okay. Promise. Obviously." She shrugged him off. "Sorry I tried to like... punch you."

His eyebrows shut up. "You were actually going to hit me?"

Her whole face went red. "No? I would have stopped myself if you didn't, obviously."

He rolled his eyes. "Go talk to your girlfriend."

Skye found Sadie and Isaac talking on the front porch. She took a deep breath and smiled before putting on her shoes and linking an arm through Sadie's.

"See you later." Skye said.

"Thanks for having me!" Sadie added.

Then neither girl talked until they'd left Isaac's street.

"I'm sorry," they said at almost the exact same time.

Skye frowned. "You didn't do anything wrong."

"You were right. I wasn't ready."

She rolled her eyes. "You were great. Totally kicked everyone's ass at monopoly."

Sadie stopped walking, staring at her feet. "I couldn't even talk," she whispered.

"Yeah, and most of them are probably hoping that'll rub off on me. It was fine. It was fun. You don't have to come back though, if you don't want to."

"I do."

Skye nodded.

"I told Isaac I'll come to the book club meeting next week in person too. She said she'll talk to Ms. Rivera about getting me a visitor's pass."

Skye frowned. "Are you—"

"Yes."

She blushed. "Right. Promise I'm working on being less paranoid. If you think it's a good idea, it'll be fine." She held out her hand. After a moment, Sadie took it and started walking again.

"I'm sorry if my friends were a lot," Skye said. "Though in all fairness, I have warned you they're assholes like, pretty much every time they come up."

Sadie shrugged. "They seemed nice. I like them."

"Trevor's cousin has like, actual autism by the way. He wasn't just randomly being an ableist dick."

"Yeah, I figured." She paused, sucking on her lip. "You told me to tell you when you do things I don't like, right?"

"Right..." Skye slowed down.

Sadie took a deep breath. "It's fine if you tell people I'm autistic, but I'd rather you let me know who you've told. You treating it like a secret felt... weird."

Skye frowned. "I didn't tell anyone anything. I don't think you're autistic, your floating thing just—"

Sadie stopped abruptly. "You didn't know I was autistic?"

That made Skye freeze too. "You are?"

"I'm... oh my god!" She started pacing across the same two sidewalk tiles, fist thumping against her side. "You thought it was just because of... I'm not going to start being normal, Skye," she told the pavement. "Even if I fully get control of the floating thing, I'm not..." She took a deep breath. "I'm bad at emotion regulation and sounds and smells and texture and stuff freak me out."

"Right, but that could be because—"

"It's not," she stopped her. "Or... it might amplify it, but I'm always going to be that way. It doesn't go away if the floating does. I've learned as many non-verbal cues as I could but I'm probably always going to be slightly awful with those and I'm bad at reading things that aren't explicit, and I hate eye contact. That's not the curse. That's me."

"I... Sadie, it's not a—"

"I mean, you don't have to deal with your emotions the way I do! How did you not... I thought if you hadn't known you must have caught on then. I can't believe I didn't—"

"Sadie." Skye grabbed her shoulder. Then hesitated for half a second, vaguely remember hearing something about people with autism not liking physical contact. Sadie was fucking obsessed with it though, so she held on. "I'm sorry I didn't know, but you need to stop expecting me to just figure things out on my own, okay? I'm apparently also very bad at non-verbal cues."

"This isn't funny."

"I didn't say it was," she said carefully. "You're... sure then? That you have it?"

She rolled her eyes. "I've seen actual hundreds of therapists. It's the kind of thing that comes up. It's not official or anything since most people qualified to diagnose do it in person after observing behavior which obviously wasn't a super viable option, but my parents kind of just started operating under the assumption that I had it after about the twentieth attempted referral."

"Okay," Skye nodded. "Good to know."

"I'm sorry I didn't tell you," she whispered. "I swear I genuinely thought you knew. I guess I'm just used to everyone around me knowing already."

Skye shrugged. "It's fine."

"No, it's not. You hit Trevor when he mentioned it."

She rolled her eyes. "Lightly. That's just how we work. And because I thought he was using it in the like, rude insulting way. Not—"

"I'm not going to stop being autistic, Skye."

"I know that."

"You freaked out when you thought he was just joking about it."

"Because I thought he was being a dick after he promised he wouldn't be. That had nothing to do with—"

"We can just be friends," she interrupted. "If you want."

Skye frowned. "I don't want to just be friends."

"You didn't sign up for any of this though. The floating or the autism or—"

"Sadie," she stopped her. "I signed up for you. I don't..." she sighed. "I don't know much about autism. I've never met anyone else with it."

"That's statistically extremely improbable. You've probably just never met anyone who told you they were autistic."

"Okay, fair, but the point is, I don't know a lot about it? Which made me fuck up today and I'm sorry about that and I'm obviously going to research it and shit, but I might fuck up again so I'm going to need you to tell me directly if I do because I'm pretty sure we've already established that I'm nowhere near as perceptive as you keep assuming I am. But I know about you. And I've liked you for years. You've been autistic that whole time so it's not like that'll suddenly change, okay?" She held out her hand again, but Sadie hesitated.

"I can be a lot," she said. "Sometimes."

"Well yeah, same. That's kind of my whole schtick. I like your lot though. More than pretty much anyone else's."

She finally smiled. "I like yours too."

Sadie

There was once a girl walking into a high school.

Hundreds of stories had started that way, probably thousands. But never hers.

She arrived before the bell when she knew the halls would be the closest to empty and walked straight to the office. Here, it truly would be dangerous to stray. And yet here was the place she most wanted to. She'd imagined herself in these rooms hundreds of times before. She couldn't help but want to fact check.

The girl walked straight to the office, announced her name, and was rewarded with a visitor's pass. A teacher walked out from the backroom and started whispering with the woman at the desk. They kept looking at her. She flicked her thumb against her knee and waited.

"Hey!"

The sometimes-floating girl almost jumped out of her own skin when someone sat down beside her.

"You good to go?"

She checked her watch. "The bell hasn't gone yet."

"It will soon," Skye Eaton shrugged.

The adults kept whispering. The sometimes-floating girl wondered how they could have possibly believed they were being subtle.

"Sadie," Skye tried again, pressing unsubtly down on her knee. "Ready to go?"

She nodded, took three deep breaths, and stood up.

"They were talking about me," the sometimes-floating girl whispered once they were in the hall.

Skye rolled her eyes. "You're cool and mysterious. Of course they were."

"What do people think about me here?"

"I don't know. That you're the most interesting thing about—"

"Skye."

She sighed. "I don't know. Honestly. There are a lot of theories."

"But there are still theories? People still talk about me?"

"We can leave," she suggested. "Right now."

"I'm fine."

Skye looked pointed down at where her toes were hovering a few centimeters off the floor.

The sometimes-floating girl sighed, flicking her side a few more times until she came back down.

"I'll be fine."

"Okay," Skye shrugged. "Let me know if that changes."

"You're supposed to be in class," the sometimes-floating girl realized. "I thought this whole thing was to make your teachers like you. That won't work if—"

"I got let out early."

The sometimes-floating girl swallowed. "Because your teachers think I'm a dying kid who needs an escort."

She frowned. "Sadie..."

"It'll be fine," she physically shook herself off. "I can deal with one needlessly pitying club supervisor."

The bell rang. The sometimes-floating girl jumped. Or perhaps she accidentally started floating for a few seconds. She'd known school bells were supposed to be loud, but she'd always thought that movies must have over exaggerated it. Skye squeezed her hand. "Okay?"

She nodded.

"Then let's go. We have a handful of reluctant teens to lecture about a book they haven't read."

Skye pulled her down the hall as it filled with students and footsteps and noise. The floating girl closed her eyes, counted to three, and tapped her hip. She took small breaths, mentally spelt "school" backwards, and squeezed Skye's fingers.

The world felt a lot smaller and more manageable once the girl was tucked away inside a classroom. She'd dreamed of exploring places like these, but perhaps that would still have to wait.

"You good?" Skye checked, slowly letting go of her hand.

The sometimes-floating girl wondered if she'd been squeezing too hard. She nodded.

The adult in the corner stood up. "Sadie," she held out a hand. "It's an honour to meet you."

The girl frowned, unsure of how to respond to that. She knew that Skye wanted to impress this adult and knew that it was therefore her job to help, but she was unaccustomed to being treated like royalty. Ms. Rivera looked about ready to bow.

"Sadie already dropped off her permission slip in the office," Skye came to her rescue. "Right, Sade?"

She nodded. Though the signature on it was the sometimes-floating girl's own. Her parents knew nothing of her newly acquired prefix yet and she hadn't known how to tell them she was going to the high school without giving that away.

Skye got to work pushing together two tables and the sometimes-floating girl moved to help. Skye caught her wrist once Ms. Rivera had returned to her desk. "If you need a notepad or computer or something—"

"I can talk."

Skye frowned at this and the sometimes-floating girl tried hard not to. She hadn't yet figured out how to explain the unpredictability of her own vocal cords.

"Cool." Skye nodded, recovering first.

One by one, her friends trickled in. The sometimes floating girl waved and cycled through "hi"s and "hello"s and "good to see you again"s. She had this. She was an expert at this. But then, all at once, in walked a stranger. And another. And another. And slowly, the sometimes-floating girl began to go fuzzy.

Skye

Skye was going to kill someone. She was going to find out who'd done this, kill them, and then find a way to resurrect them just to kill them again.

But for now, she had to get her girlfriend out of the room.

"Sadie." She grabbed both of her hands. She didn't know if that would help or hurt since she knew Sadie normally needed to move her arms when she got overwhelmed, but it felt better than just letting her float away. She kept her fingers light in case Sadie had to pull away but when she didn't, Skye pushed down.

"We have the room booked!" She announced. It sounded like yelling. Skye had always been good at yelling.

Dozens of confused faces stared at her, but none of them moved.

"So get the fuck out!" She added. Then, remembering Ms. Rivera, tacked on a "please."

Ms. Rivera got up from her desk. "They're supposed to be here, Skye. I figured it'd be more fun to get some new recruits."

Skye's body went hot. Not today. This would have almost been fine, any meeting but today. But, she realized, that was probably why people had suddenly bothered showing up.

"They didn't even read the book," she pointed out. People were starting to sit down. She needed to stop them before they sat down.

Ms. Rivera frowned. "I'm sure it'll still be a worthwhile conversation."

"But—"

She sighed. "We've been over this, Skye. You can't run a public outreach club if you refuse to involve the public."

Her arms we tugged up. She stomped down on Sadie's foot. "Are we going?" She checked.

Sadie nodded, so she pulled her out the door. She wasn't sure if she was attached enough to the ground to walk on her own.

"Okay," Skye panted, pulling her into the nearest open classroom and locking the door behind them. She started looking for something to block the window with but the moment she let go on Sadie's hands, she was already drifting up. "Can you do your thing?" She asked. "Move around or whatever until you come down?"

Sadie flapped her wrists. She shook her torso. "I can't."

Skye frowned. "Is it not working? Maybe we weren't right about—"

"I don't know what I'm supposed to do!" She yelled.

Skye stared. Unlike her own, Sadie's yelling always carried weight.

"I can feel that I'm supposed to be doing something, but I don't know how... no one ever told me what to do!"

"Okay," Skye said slowly, raising her hands in surrender as she stepped closer. "take a deep breath and—"

"I've been doing that my whole life! It doesn't..." her hand twitched at her side. "It doesn't work for me! Nothing ever gets to be that fucking easy for me!"

She was crying. Maybe that was what did it. Or maybe it was the crying and yelling or the crying and yelling and hand twitching but suddenly, she was descending again. She buried her face in her knees.

Skye sat down cross-legged across from her. "Sadie..." she reached out to touch her then pulled her hand back. She wasn't sure how to deal with a Sadie who screamed. She sighed. "I thought it would just be us. I'm sorry."

"They came to see me, didn't they? To look at me?"

"I think so. You're pretty cool to look at though, so—"

"Skye."

She winced. "I know. I'm sorry, I don't know how to help here."

Sadie was quiet. Hugging her knees and swaying and whispering something under her breath. She had no idea how to deal with any of that.

"I'll be back, okay? I'll go try and kick everyone out."

Because even if she didn't know what to do, there was one thing she'd always been amazing at: getting mad.

Skye stormed back to the room and threw open the door. Isaac was writing something on the board. She wasn't sure what. She was pretty sure she didn't even bother keeping track of whatever books they were all pretending to read anymore. Everyone's attention moved to Skye when the door hit the wall.

"Everyone out," she grumbled. "Club's cancelled."

Ms. Rivera frowned, getting up from her desk. "Is every—"

"Everyone get the fuck out! She's not coming back, okay? Leave!"

There was silence, then shuffling. The packing of backpacks. The fleeing of feet. Her friends hovered near the door, but she glared at them. "Out."

And then she was alone with an English teacher.

Ms. Rivera pushed up her reading classes. "I don't appreciate you pre-emptively ending my club."

"It's my club. You just sit there."

She sighed. "This was always a public club, Skye. You can't get upset that—"

"It's a fucking book club. None of those people were here to talk about books."

She raised an eyebrow. "Were you?"

She'd seen through her, then. Maybe she'd always known.

"You should have warned me you were inviting people," Skye grumbled.

"I thought you'd appreciate the help. You clearly couldn't get people on—"

"I did the fucking announcements. No one wanted to come."

"You made it sound like just another book club. I knew if—"

"It is just another book club!" Skye's fists shook. She took a step towards the centre of the room, distancing herself from anything throwable. She felt her heart hammer and for a moment, Ms. Rivera was smart enough to look afraid.

She turned back towards her desk to gather her things. "I think we're done here."

Skye nodded. That was probably for the best. "Next week there'd better not be—"

"I meant for good, Skye." She adjusted the strap on her laptop case, walking past her to the door. "We both know this was barely a club to begin with."

Skye gritted her teeth together. "Fine." She'd come up with another plan. She always came up with a plan.

Ms. Rivera stopped in the doorway and turned around. She sighed again. "I think you're a good kid, Skye. I appreciate what you were trying to do for your friend. But if you were intentionally trying to keep the club small so she didn't—"

"Sadie didn't ask me to do that."

She frowned. "The point is, that's the kind of thing you could have talked to me about privately instead of lashing out. We can give it one last shot, if you apologize and show me that you're willing to compromise this time."

She stared at her. If there was one thing Skye Eaton was good at, it was apologizing. She'd grown up on "I'm sorry"s, both real and fake. It was practically second nature.

She picked up her bag, slung it over her shoulder, and wordlessly walked out.

Sadie

There was once a sometimes-floating girl who was never supposed to float in the first place. There was once a sometimes-floating girl who'd spent a lifetime accidentally building the art of going fuzzy into her very bones. There was once a girl who might not have ever needed to float, but now, she was always seconds away from being on the ceiling.

She closed her eyes and counted. She rocked and she tapped. But every time the sometimes-floating girl got close to the floor, she would falter. She'd imagine walking out of that room into a world where everyone would watch for each tap or sway or twitch and go back up to the ceiling.

She was half-sick of ceilings.

So, she self-destructed. She came unwound in a flurry of fists and hums. She pounded the ceiling then the walls then herself then the ground. She stomped and shook and cried and screamed.

The sometimes-floating girl remained grounded, but at what cost?

The true evil of her curse had always been just that: that it was a curse. That it was selective. That, as far as the sometimes-floating girl knew, no one else ever had to stomp or shake or cry or scream to remain on the ground. The floating itself was not scary, it was a mere minor inconvenience. The sometimes-floating girl's truest enemy was a non-floating person looking up, catching sight of her up there against the sky, and finally realizing what she had always known: that the suffix didn't matter.

There was never a girl who floated. Girls were not built for the sky. So, if the floating was undeniable, then the fault must have lied in the end of the title.

There was once a sometimes-floating-something. There was sometimes a floating nothing. There was sometimes a hurricane of a girl attacking the ground but then, that didn't feel quite human either, did it?

Skye

When she got back to the classroom she'd left Sadie in, it was empty.

Skye: whr r u?
Skye: Sadie.
Skye: r u okay?
Skye: Sadie?
Skye: Sadie
Skye: Sadie
Skye: Sadie
Skye: Sadie
Skye: Sadie
Skye: Sadie
Skye: Sadie
Skye: Sadie
Skye: Sadie
Skye: Sadie
Skye: Sadie
Skye: Sadie
Skye: Sadie
Skye: Sadie
Skye: Sadie
Skye: Sadie
Skye: Sadie
Skye: Sadie
Skye: Sadie
Skye: Sadie
Skye: Sadie
Skye: Sadie
Skye: Sadie
Skye: Sadie
Skye: Sadie
Skye: Sadie
Skye: Sadie
Skye: Sadie

Sadie

There were several times a heroic human. There was often a heroic human. Sometimes the human was flawed too, but there was often a heroic human.

There were sometimes heroic animals. Or flawed animals. But they weren't really animals, were they? They were metaphors. Animal shells with the souls of humans stuffed inside them.

There were heroic humans and flawed humans and heroic animal shaped humans and flawed animal shaped humans.

What there wasn't, what there never were, were human shaped somethings.

Skye

She went to her house. She almost knocked. But while Skye was absolutely fucking oblivious about a lot of things, she'd already figured out that Sadie hadn't told her parents about visiting the school that day. She just hadn't said anything because she'd really wanted her to come.

She walked up and down the driveway once more then got on her bike and rode away.

Sadie

There was once a nothing.

Some people avoided the nothing and its cool, unknowable darkness. Some threw gifts and offerings at it, thinking pity and sympathy could fill it back up.

Then came a girl who threw screams and planes. The nothing decided it liked the way that tasted so when she came back, it drudged years of human trinkets up to the surface to try and convince her that they were one and the same.

The nothing had a use for the girl. Or maybe, the girl had a use for it. The nothing had always known that, but it continued coughing up all that it could.

But nothings cannot pretend to be human. Not forever. That wasn't how it worked.

Skye

She biked to Isaac's because she wasn't ready to bike home. They were all there waiting for her, because they knew her better than she knew herself. She hovered in the doorway.

"Sorry," she said. "If I lost it for a few seconds there." She checked her phone again, but the screen was still blank. "I don't know where she went," she whispered.

They let her in.

She sat on her favourite couch and denied offerings of search parties because Sadie wasn't a lost dog, she was just a girl who was sad. Or mad at her, but Skye had always been a worst-case scenario kind of person.

She couldn't tell them that maybe she was just stuck up somewhere, waiting to come down. She couldn't say that she wasn't worried she was missing, because she wasn't. Sadie said she never went dangerously high, and she trusted that. But Skye knew she'd feel like shit if she wasn't there when she came back down again.

But she'd clearly left the building without telling her, so maybe she wouldn't want her there anyway.

She pressed her head against her knees. "I fucked up."

No one denied it. She wouldn't have been friends with them if they weren't honest.

Isaac sat down beside her and wrapped an arm around her back. "You'll fix it," she decided.

And so, she would.

Sadie

The nothing went home.

She didn't, at first. She stopped in her favourite patch of forest where she could scream and punch and shake as much as she wanted to. She unwound until there wasn't enough breath left in her lungs for floating or crying. Then, the nothing went home.

Her parents were on the couch. They both jumped up when the door closed behind her. The nothing was rarely ever gone as long as she had been.

"What happened?" Her mother asked.

Maybe there was mud on her jeans or dirt in her hair or a little too much nothingness in her eyes.

The nothing blinked. "When was the first time I floated?"

She'd never asked. She'd always just assumed. Surely if she hadn't been cursed pre-birth, her parents would have let her know. It would have come up.

Her parents looked at each other and the nothing instantly knew that it hadn't intentionally.

"You were three," her father said. "I think."

As if a suddenly floating child was something he would have been able to forget.

The nothing's fist slammed against her side. She raced to her bedroom and piled her covers high to try and keep herself together.

Skye: I'm sorry today was a mess

Skye: hope you're doing okay

Skye: let me know if you're up to talk

Nonymous

Sadie

There was once a nothing who convinced a girl that she was something. There was once a girl who deserved to know the truth.

Sadie: *meet me at the entrance to the trail down the street from my house in an hour.*

Skye

It was less dark than the first time she'd met Sadie there. Colder too. Skye shoved her fists into her pockets while she waited, wishing she'd worn something heavier.

Sadie (who was always wearing something heavy) arrived jacketless in a short-sleeved dress. She kept her eyes near the earth. "Hi," she said.

"Hi," Skye said back. "Are you... you're okay? Today was such a mess. If I'd known—"

"I'm not a public service project."

She frowned, taking a step back. "I... yeah. I know, obviously."

"Your teacher called your club a public service project."

She sighed, reaching towards her. "Sadie, I—"

She stepped back. "Do you know why I emailed you back?" She asked. "When we were kids?"

"N—"

"My entire life, everyone's always treated me like I was broken. Teachers and therapists and social workers and doctors and my own freaking parents... you didn't do that. You were entitled and abrasive and rude and I needed... I was sick of people talking about me like I was more of a problem then a person."

She reached for her. "Sadie..."

"Stop doing that!" She jumped back. "Stop saying my name like even that makes you sad! I'm not... I don't... just stop it!"

Her feet were already at Skye's knees.

"Sade, you're—"

"I know," she squeezed her eyes shut, but then reopened them just as quickly when Skye grabbed her hand to try and help pull her down. "Don't do that!"

Skye jumped away. "I—I'm sorry?"

"I'm not going to start being normal Skye. I'm not going to magically... I'm always going to do this! You weren't supposed to treat me like some thing you can fix. I never asked... I'm never going to be fixable!"

Skye frowned. "You did!" She didn't know if she was yelling because she was mad or because Sadie was getting so high that she was worried her words would get lost in the air. "You're the one who asked!"

If Sadie responded, she was too high for Skye to hear her.

So, Skye Eaton, student nothing, began to climb.

Sadie

There was once a nothing at war with her atoms.

She'd cloaked herself in thin, breezy cotton because for the first time she could remember, the nothing had set out determined to trick no one of her truest nature. She hovered against the dark—not the highest she'd ever risen. Not by far—fist thumping against her side, but floating still. She'd planned on coming up here. She'd set off knowing that she was skybound. She simply hadn't accounted for the cold.

She'd meant to stay up until Skye Eaton left, but then gooseflesh overtook her arms and she decided to come down and found that she couldn't. She'd made the mistake of panicking. Her body still hadn't learned how to toe the line between embracing and fleeing from panic, so she thumped and thumped and was hyperaware of it all the while. Perhaps that was why it didn't work.

"Take the jacket."

If she was a person, she would have jumped. Instead, the nothing spun around to meet the sound she'd assumed had just been a squirrel hiding away from the night air. A girl's face stared at her from a tree, arm and jacket extended between them.

She wrapped her hands around her shaking arms. "I don't want it."

"I know. That's why I didn't ask if you wanted it. Take the fucking jacket."

She did, careful not to drop it as she pulled it around her shoulders. They sat—and hovered—in silence.

"You climbed a tree," the nothing said.

"Yeah. And I have absolutely no upper body strength, so it's extra impressive."

"I didn't ask you to do that."

The girl in the tree shrugged. "I know. You did ask me to help stop the floating though, for the record. I was originally coming up here to yell at you about that."

"And now?"

"Now? Now I just spent ten minutes climbing a fucking tree, so I need a bit of time to work my way back up to pissed."

The nothing didn't know what to say to that. She rarely ever did.

The tree girl sighed. "It wasn't supposed to be an outreach club or anything, just so you know. It was just going to be a sham attempt at getting a university referral. I asked you to join before we switched to the outreach route because I liked you and wanted to trick you into spending more time with me. We only let Ms. Rivera think that was what it was because it was the easiest way to get her to okay the club."

"I'm not a pity project." The nothing told the clouds.

"I know, obviously. You were helping me, not the other way around. That's why it felt like such a non-thing that I didn't bother mentioning it to you."

"You didn't mention it because you knew I wouldn't like it." The nothing was tired of people pretending she never knew what was going on. Just because she entered the air sometimes didn't mean she couldn't still see the ground.

Skye sighed. "Okay, yeah. Maybe. Sorry, okay? I should have told you."

"I would have went along with it. If you'd asked me to."

"I know. I fucked up, you can be mad about that. But you don't get to be pissed at me for doing something you asked me to do."

"I didn't mean..." The nothing squeezed her eyes shut, counted to three, and kept floating. "I like being on the ground."

Skye laughed nervously. "Yeah, as someone currently trusting a bit of wood to keep me from plummeting towards it, kind of get the appeal."

"It's not like that though. I'm not in danger when I float, I'm just... higher up. It's obviously more convenient to stay on the ground, but I don't think I'm ever going to be able to do that permanently." She scratched at her tights. "I was right. It didn't start until I was three."

"Shit," Skye said.

"And maybe if things had been different then or if they'd just let it happen then I would have it under control by now, but I don't. It's not just going to suddenly go away and even if it does, it's so, so, hard to hold onto the ground sometimes. I can't just do that all the time. I don't think..." she sighs. "It's not fixable. I was only supposed to come tonight to prove it wasn't fixable."

"Good to know."

"I can keep coming to your club virtually if you need me to. But if you're going to use me, I'd rather you be upfront about—"

"I was never using you."

The nothing frowned. "I said I'd keep coming. I'm not mad if—"

"No, fuck that. I am. What the hell, Sadie?"

"I'm... I don't know—"

"You've known me for basically ever and you seriously think I was using you for some club I don't even give a shit about? That I wasn't even planning on starting until less than two months ago?"

The nothing cock her head to the side. "You didn't know about all this back then either. I'm not..." she untangled her tongue. "I didn't mean to imply that I thought you'd been pretending to like me the whole time, but after you found out that I—"

"That you can fly?"

"That I sometimes float," she corrected. "You didn't find out until after we'd agreed to date and after you needed to use me for your club and that..." she shook her head. Not because she was trying to say no, but because something needed to match her shaking voice. "That changed things. Not even just that. You didn't know about the autism or the anxiety or... none of that's going away either. Or maybe... there's so much wrong with me that I don't know where all of it comes from. Big groups of people might freak me out because I'm not used to them because of the floating but it also could be the autism or... maybe I get used to somethings and get better at dealing with that, but it's never all going to go away. And you didn't know any of that."

Skye rolled her eyes. "Believe it or not, my ability to like you isn't based off of how much you love crowds of other people. It's—"

"You don't get it!" The nothing exclaimed. "I'm never going to fix this! I either get emotional and float or get emotional and stim but no matter what, I'm never going to magically be good at being human!"

Skye frowned. "You're not actually a ghost, you know that, right? Or an alien or mutant or robot?"

She sighed. "I know, I'm just... I'm not normal either."

"Who the hell is?"

"You know what I mean."

Skye rolled her eyes. "I'm so bad at pretending to be normal that I had to invent a whole club just to try and trick an adult into thinking I was decent enough to sign a paper. No one's normal, some people are just less shit at pretending to be."

The nothing swallowed. "That's not the same thing. You don't... most people's not normals and my not normals are always going to be really, really different."

"I know," Skye admitted. "Doesn't mean yours is any worse though."

She sighed. "Skye."

She sighed back. "Sadie."

"I'm in the middle of the air right now. That's not..."

"It's awesome."

The nothing squinted at her. She did not appreciate being lied to.

"Seriously. I've only been acting like it's not because you don't act like it is and you obviously get to take point on how we're supposed to react to your own shit. If it's upsetting you obviously I don't like it either, but it's only ever bothered me because it bothers you."

The nothing frowned. "Promise?"

"Yes. Absolutely."

She felt the fuzziness decrease, but she couldn't go down. Not yet. "I still like you," she blurted, desperate to say it before she was too far away.

Skye laughed. "Good. I still like you too. Lots."

"I think I'm about to abandon you in a tree."

"Got it." She nodded. "Meet you on the ground."

The nothing got down first, despite how gradually she floated. Skye Eaton was truly awful at climbing trees. She waited on the ground for her then held out a hand and declared, "I'd like to keep being girlfriends. If you would."

"Okay," Skye smiled, accepting the handshake.

"I'm still going to try and keep from floating."

"Cool. I liked you before knowing you could do that anyways."

"It might still happen though."

"Also cool."

"And I'm not..." she sucked on her lip. "I'm never going to be as good at pretending to be normal as everyone else. I'm never going to be the kind of girlfriend who can do cute surprise dates or dances or parties. I'm always going to be too easy to overwhelm and too emotional and never—"

"Sadie." Skye stepped closer. "You feel things strongly enough to defy physics. How the fuck am I supposed to see that as anything less than incredible?"

She kissed her and the nothing decided that maybe nothing didn't fit either. Surely nothing would not be able to feel this many somethings all at once. So maybe she was something or nothing or everything or somewhere in-between. Maybe she was girl or floating or neither or both. But mostly, she was Sadie O'Brian, in a forest, being kissed.

Skye

"You shouldn't have cancelled your club," Sadie told her as they walked back together, hand in hand. "That was stupid."

Skye blushed. "To be fair, I'm pretty sure I'm not the one who cancelled it."

"I'm sorry. I know the reference thing was important to you."

She shrugged. "If I needed to fake an entire club to get in, maybe I shouldn't get in. My grades are fine, I'll get in somewhere no matter what. Not all programs need references."

"Still. That sucks."

"I still have time to convince one of my other teachers this semester that I'm reformed enough or whatever to sign off on. I'll just have to get better at you know, not saying the first thing that comes to mind every second for like a month?"

"Good thing I happen to know way more self-regulation tricks than one person could possibly ever need."

Skye grinned. "See? They'll love me in no time."

Sadie paused at the end of her driveway. "I don't know if I want to deal with my parents right now."

"You can come hide out at my place."

"No," she shook herself out. "I should talk to them."

"I can come help yell at them."

The corners of her mouth ticked up, but she shook her head again. "I'm not going to yell at them."

"You could. I'd—"

"I'm not you though. I'm not mad. I'm just... I don't know what I am. I have to do this my own way though."

Skye nodded. She let go of her hand and stepped back. "Okay," she said. "Text me if you need back up? Or even if you don't, text me anyways?"

She smiled, handing her back her jacket. "I can do that."

Sadie

There was once Sadie O'Brian, slipping in through her back door. Her parents normally went to bed fairly early, but she'd already known that they'd both been there waiting for her.

"You're awake," she pointed out anyway.

They both stared at her. "We went to say goodnight and you weren't in your room," her father said.

She nodded. "I was with Skye."

They looked at each other. They did not seem surprised.

Sadie shook out her wrists. She swayed from side to side. "I've been figuring out how to stay on the ground."

That did surprise them.

"What—" her mother started, in tandem with her father's "how—"

Explaining was hard, but she's seen that coming. She pulled out her phone.

It turns out I just have to let myself feel things the way my body wants to feel things. It's not being emotional that causes it, it's forcing myself to pretend I'm not.

"That's... that's wonderful," her mother said. "We're glad you're figuring out how to cope, sweetheart. But you still need to be careful about—"

She held up a hand to stop her. She deleted. She retyped. *Did you guys already know?*

"What?"

She knew that they could both read. They didn't really need her to repeat herself. She tapped at the screen.

Did you guys already know?

"Sadie," her father said. "If we'd known how to help, we would have already, sweetheart."

But I didn't always do this, she typed. Her fingers felt too hot against the screen even though her phone hadn't been on long enough to overheat. *You knew it couldn't have just been caused by emotions. I cried as a baby and nothing happened.*

They looked at each other again. They used their secret language as if she wasn't standing right there.

"Sadie," her father began. She had already decided that she didn't want to hear whatever message they'd decided on. She was sick of them keeping things from her. "Just because we couldn't figure out exactly what caused it doesn't mean we were keeping anything from you. It seemed like it was your emotions. It still sounds like it kind of is. Of course that's how we tried to handle it."

She felt tears—hot and fast and angry—start to escape her eyes. Her swaying picked up speed and her free arm started to flap, but for once, she pushed down the voice at the back of her head telling her to stay still. She wanted to be level with them for this conversation. She watched them watch her. She watched them look away. She started typing again.

Would you rather I do this or float?

They looked at each other again.

She deleted and retyped, though she could barely see the screen anymore.

Are you more afraid of people seeing me float or knowing I'm autistic?

She heard her mother gasp and suddenly, there were two pairs of arms around her.

Sadie decided right there that when she was like this—sad or mad or any kind of overwhelmed—she didn't want to be hugged. No matter how the person meant it, it would always feel too much like they were trying keep her from floating or flapping or flying. Her voice was not working and her arms were too trapped to type though, so she'd have to wait to establish that later. She waited until her parents' grips were loose enough for her to shake herself free. She sat down—for she could have conversations like this sitting now—and waited for her parents to follow suit.

"No one's ashamed of you, sweetie," her mother said. She wondered if she knew she was giving herself away there, through jumping right to shame. She wondered if her mother even knew that that's what she was feeling. "The world's just not... it can be mean sometimes, honey. To people like you."

They had proof of no other floating girls, so Sadie knew exactly what "people like you" meant.

"We love you exactly how you are, we just don't want the rest of the world to judge you for it."

People made the mistake, sometimes, of thinking that fairy tales were sugar-coated. They called them unrealistic for their happy endings because they didn't know that most fairy tales didn't end happily. Fairy tales weren't stories of human successes, they were cautionary tales against human failure and cruelty. Sadie had never once been as naïve about the rest of the world as everyone around her seemed to think.

I am going to start going out more, she typed.

"Okay."

On my own.

"Are you sure that's a good idea?"

No, she wrote. *But I'm going to do it anyway.* She hesitated, trying to puzzle out what to say. *You're allowed to be worried about me,* she wrote. *But I need you not to be worried at me. Floating or stimming or doing whatever I want to do in the moment are always going to be parts of me and if you always act scared of that, I'm never going to figure out how to be fine with it myself. You can't stop the rest of the world from judging me by beating them to it.*

They both reached for her again, but when she backed into the cushion, their arms dropped. Maybe they somehow already knew. Hopefully, she'd never have to tell them.

"Sadie," her father started again, eyes full of sympathy and pity and a million less identifiable things.

She held out a hand to stop him again. *All I need you to say right now is okay.*

"Okay," he said. He looked towards her mother.

"Okay." She confirmed.

Sadie nodded. She started typing again. She figured it was best to get this all done at once.

Also, I like girls.

Her parents' eyes exchanged another secret message but this time, they were fighting down smiles as they did so.

"Yes, dear," her mother said. "we know."

Skye's my girlfriend.

Her father's eyes widened. He put a hand over his mouth. "Good for her."

Sadie got up to go to her bedroom. Her feet made contact with each and every stair.

Skye

"If you want to leave you have to let me know right away so we can go together," Skye said. "We can have a secret code or something."

They'd finished studying at her place that morning and were on their way to Isaac's.

Sadie (whose hand was in Skye's) rolled her eyes. "You don't have to leave if I decide to."

"I absolutely do. I'm shit at Catan and only agreed to play because they said we could be a team. The secret code's for me, not for you."

"I could just say I want to go?"

Skye nodded. "That works too." She shoved her free hand into her pocket.

Sadie frowned. "You're nervous."

"What? No, I'm—"

"Your voice is getting all fast and high."

Skye sighed.

"If you get to always see when I'm overwhelmed, I get to memorize your tells too."

"Okay, fine. Fair. I've just really fucked up both of the other times you've met them in person? I'm just paranoid I'll do something stupid again."

"I promise to tell you if you do."

Skye laughed. "That's... actually extremely helpful. Thank you."

Sadie squeezed her fingers. "It'll be fine."

And it was. They played two rounds and won one and although the conversation occasionally got slightly stilted like it did every time they tried to add a new person to their dynamic, it felt a lot calmer than their last game night. Hopefully, they'd keep inching their way towards casual. Everything was normal and fine and mistake free so when everyone went to leave and Isaac said, "can I steal Skye for a bit?" she had no idea what she'd done wrong.

Sadie just nodded and went to go wait upstairs.

"What—" Skye started back towards the couches. Isaac grabbed her arm.

"Are you staying here?"

"I'm walking Sadie home," she said. "And I have a lot of work to do tomorrow so—"

"Not in my house, in town."

She frowned. "What? No. Just because the book club thing didn't work out doesn't mean I'm absolutely hopeless. Even if I don't get into my first choices, I'll find somewhere else nearby and we'll still split our shitty little basement apartment."

She sighed. "You're in love with her, Skye. Full heart eyes and everything."

Skye blushed. She neither confirmed nor denied the accusation. "That doesn't mean we're not going to Toronto. Sadie's going to be a writer. She can do that anywhere."

"She's not leaving town next year."

"She might."

Isaac ran a hand through her hair. "She just started leaving her house regularly for the first time, Skye. You can't drag her all the way to Toronto."

She didn't have a response for that.

Isaac sighed. "I love you, I want you to be happy, but I need to know what the plan is so I can figure out what I'm doing next year, okay?"

She swallowed. "We're going. That's always been... we're going."

"Okay," she nodded. "Awesome. Just... let me know if that changes?"

"It won't."

Isaac watched her. "If you'd rather go somewhere closer and don't let yourself because of some half-baked plan we made at fifteen, I'll actually kill you."

"Noted." Skye glanced towards the stairs. "I'm not changing my mind," she said slowly. "But if I do, it's not because I'm choosing her over you, you know that, right? You're—"

Isaac groaned, shoving her towards the steps. "Go be sappy with your girlfriend. This feels gross."

She cackled the whole way up.

"Hey." She found Sadie sitting on Isaac's porch. "You good to go?"

She stood up. "Everything okay?"

"What? Yeah. She just wanted to talk about plans for next year."

"When you move away," she clarified.

Skye started to walk down the driveway. "Yeah, and then you—" she froze when she realized she was alone but when she turned around, Sadie was still on the ground. "are you—"

"I can't live in Toronto," she blurted out. "I know I made it sound like I could, but I can't... maybe I could eventually, but I'm still getting used to being around smaller crowds of people here and it sounds like a sensory nightmare and I don't—"

"Sadie," she lightly touched her arm. "It's okay. I think I kind of already knew that. We'll figure it out." She hesitated. "But I can't... I like you, a lot, but I think I need to go. Even if I don't get into a good program there, I have to go somewhere." She sighed. "I like you and I like being with you, but I've spent so much of my life working towards getting somewhere bigger and queerer and easier to blend into and I think I need to see that through. At least for a bit. At least until I figure out what kind of person I can be there."

Sadie frowned. "I wasn't going to ask you to stay."

"I know. You wouldn't." She took her hand again. "We still have until the end of summer. And then I'll be home a lot anyways to visit my parents or you could come visit us if you ever decide you're comfortable with that and we could obviously video chat and text and call all the time. And I'd probably be back in the

summers. If you're comfortable doing long distance, obviously,"
she quickly added. "If you're not—"

Sadie stepped closer to her. So close that she swore she
could feel her breath on her forehead. "I'm extremely okay with
long distance," she said. "I've met some of my favourite people
that way."

Sadie kissed her. They'd been doing that a lot, recently.
When it happened there was no tongue bashing or teeth hitting
and it wasn't middle school or high school or college or maybe it
was all of the above. They'd been doing it so much recently, that
Skye's brain was too desensitized to overthink it. Her heart didn't
pound and it wasn't exciting or dramatic or terrifying, it was just
warm. Calm. And when she opened her eyes, they were both still
on the ground.

Sadie

There was once an author on her way back from a young writer's workshop.

It was her fourth time there; the library held them every week. Attendance was so low that "young" had been extended to mean anything from middle school to mid twenties and even then, there were never more than a dozen people in attendance.

Sadie O'Brian had decided that she loved libraries the minute she'd first walked into one. If it were up to her, they'd meet nightly.

She, her notebook, and her laptop made the walk home together. The workshop didn't end until nine-thirty and her parents kept offering to drive her, but she was trying to get them more used to her being out alone in the dark. Sneaking out was exciting, but it was far from convenient.

Snow started to fall in light flurries as she walked. She stuck out her tongue to catch a flake just as her phone buzzed in her pocket.

Skye: *Surprise! I'm taking you on a super romantic surprise date!*

Skye: *It is, unfortunately, at a Denny's. Gotta save up for uni so I didn't want to set the bar too high*

Skye: *Butttt I went in today and bullied them into making a reservation. Super cool surprise date's next Friday at 7, we're sitting here. I'll send you the address*

She waited for the grainy picture of a crudely circled booth to come through before slipping her phone back into her pocket.

Then, grinning ear to ear, Sadie O'Brian jumped up and down in the moonlight.

Nonymous

Nonymous

Author's Note & Acknowledgement

Quick reminder that straight/cis/allo/allistic aren't defaults and unless one of my characters explicitly states their identity to you, they have no canon identity. They're teens and might not have all facets of their identities figured out yet. While I've been careful to market this as an ace & autistic book instead of an ace-autistic one as neither girl uses both labels, that doesn't necessarily mean that neither could. Especially in books like this where they both express little previous understanding of each other's labels.

Thank you as always to all of my lovely early readers for helping me with this one! This would have been so much harder without the help of Sofa, Sarah A., El H., Maddie G., L. Brennan, Meadow Bush, Ace Huisman, Sophia V., Zeynep Y., Berry, Anjuga, Catie, Chelsea K., Amy Taylor, Onyx Wylde, KD, SG and Kathryn!

I want to highlight that both Sadie & Skye have spectrum identities. If you identify or were considering identifying as ace/autistic and don't line up with their experiences of that, it doesn't mean you might not also be on those spectrums. Similarly, Sadie's not a diagnostic guide, she's a character. Relating to her doesn't automatically mean you have ASD. Identity's complex and messy and ace and autism rep are hard to come across so if this is one of the first times you've encountered either, please don't take either of my characters as representative of an entire community.

Finally, thanks for you, to reading. And for reading the acknowledgements. Most people don't get this far :)

Nonymous

About The Author

Alex (any pronouns) published their first book a month after
turning 20 then decided publishing a book a month for 10 months
after that was a reasonable goal. AND GUESS WHAT! IT WAS!
YOU JUST FINISHED READING BOOK TEN! He will
henceforth never be calm about anything ever again.

Alex has become addicted to this and is currently working towards
publishing 22 sapphic books before turning 22. To join her reader
list and get 1 email a month with info on new and upcoming
releases, early reader opportunities, genre polls, and other polls
(Alex really likes polls), message them at
alexnonymouswrites@gmail.com

See you next month
:)

CWS: Swearing (lots of it), negative self-talk, (implied) autistic
meltdown (non graphic/descriptive from within character's head)